FRIDAY

E. L. TODD

D1439799

Fallen Publishing

Friday

CHAPTER ONE

The Fool

Marie

I never felt so stupid in my entire life.

When we were in bed together, I wasn't thinking clearly. I was doing what I always did—feeling. Every time he moved inside me and kissed me, I felt something. It was more than just physical desire or a pleasurable touch. It meant something so much more. I was a flower and he was my sun. I was the lamb and he was the wolf. Maybe I shouldn't have said what I said but I couldn't help it.

I meant it.

I never expected him to get up and leave like that. He stormed out and didn't look back. When I asked him to stay he refused. For some idiotic reason, I thought he felt what I did. I thought something developed over these past few months, and not just something insignificant.

I thought he loved me too.

Not only was I embarrassed for putting myself out there like that. But I was also hurt.

Actually, I was broken.

I went to class like everything was normal and concentrated on my schoolwork. When I was at The Grind, I focused on making coffee and keeping the place clean.

But of course, my mind drifted to him.

What did this mean? Were we done? Just like that?

A whole week went by and I didn't hear a peep from him. Since he was the one who left, I refused to contact him first. I may be heartbroken over what he did, but I wasn't so desperate.

Axel was an honorable man who was always honest. If he didn't love me, he wouldn't say it just to make me happy. But I didn't think he was the type of guy to take off without saying another word. It was cold, to say the least.

With every passing day it was difficult for me to put on a brave face and pretend everything was all right. When I was around Francesca I did my best to appear normal. I didn't want to dump my emotional shit on Francesca—especially when it was about Axel.

Francesca just pulled out a batch of muffins from the oven. They smelled like apple cinnamon, and they made our house smell like a bakery. No matter how delicious their scent was, it couldn't mask the stench of my pain.

She set the pan on the counter and waited for them to cool. "It's weird not seeing Axel around." She picked the top of a muffin and popped a chunk into her mouth.

"Yeah, he's busy." I sat at the kitchen table with my laptop open. I had a ten-page paper due and I only had a single paragraph done. And the introduction was always the easiest part.

"Too busy for you?" She chuckled like that was absurd. "Not possible."

Axel used to be so sweet to me. He was at my beck-and-call, and even when I needed a break he refused to leave my side. He slept with me every night and found any reason to kiss me. I missed the way he looked at me, like I was his whole world.

How did I misread him?

Francesca scooped out a muffin and set it on a plate before she passed it to me. "Something wrong?"

Friday

"No." I said it quickly and kept my gaze averted. I pulled the muffin toward me because I was in desperate need of comfort food.

Francesca continued to stand at the table, and she tilted her head slightly to get a good look at me. "Are you sure? You've been super quiet lately."

"Just stressed with school...semester is almost over."

Francesca knew me better than anyone, so she knew when I was full of shit. "Seriously, what's wrong? You've been weird lately and I thought you were just tired or something but it's been going on a while...what aren't you telling me?"

I didn't want to keep it from her. I told her everything, and having that kind of friendship always made me feel better. But since Axel was her brother, it was just awkward. "Nothing."

She pulled out the chair and plopped down into it. "Don't bullshit with me. What is it?"

I picked at the muffin and felt the crumbles in my fingers.

"Girl, tell me. I can tell there's something on your mind." She stared at me hard and waited for a response.

"It's Axel...I think we broke up."

She couldn't hold back her gasp. "What? Seriously? How?"

I shrugged. "He walked out and that's the end of the story."

"He walked out? What does that mean? Marie, start from the top." The TV was on in the background but we both forgot it was there.

I sighed and kept picking at the muffin. "It's awkward..."

"You can still tell me. I won't be weird about it."

"Well, it *should* weird you out."

She snapped her fingers in my face. "I'm a mature adult. Marie, you're my best friend and I need to know these things—even if it concerns my brother."

"Well...we were together..."

She knew exactly what I meant but didn't make a face. "Okay. What else?"

"And I said something I shouldn't..." I was mortified at the memory.

"What did you say?"

"I love you."

Her eyes widened. "You did?"

I nodded, feeling dumber by the second.

"And what happened? He didn't say it back?"

"He stopped what he was doing, got dressed, and left."

Francesca cupped her mouth and gasped so loud it was practically a scream. "Oh my god."

I pushed the muffin aside because now I had no appetite.

"Are you serious?" she snapped. "He just left? He walked out on you?"

I nodded.

"That fucking asshole."

Despite how upset I was I couldn't call him that.

"Have you spoken to him?"

I shook my head. "I haven't called or texted. He hasn't either."

"How long has it been?"

"A week."

"That's unbelievable."

I nodded, unsure what else to do.

"I still can't believe that. You tell him you love him and he takes off? Jackass."

He definitely didn't look good.

"And he doesn't call or explain himself? That's it? It's just...over?"

"I guess." There was always a possibility this relationship would fail, but I assumed it would end better than this. What we had was too meaningful for a wordless goodbye. He dropped me like I didn't mean anything to him, like my feelings didn't matter. My heart had never been broken like this.

"Wow...I'm going to give him a piece of my mind."

"I appreciate it but stay out of it." There wasn't much to stay out of, actually. "I feel stupid for ever thinking we would go somewhere. I thought he was different but it turns out I was wrong...he never changed."

When Francesca saw the sadness in my eyes she scooted the chair closer to me then wrapped her arms around me. She gave me the affection I needed, the embrace I'd been longing for. "Marie, it'll be okay."

Now I understood how Francesca felt when Hawke left. I wasn't losing my mind or becoming suicidal but I was devastated. I knew how I felt about him before he left, but now that he was gone I understood something else.

He was the love of my life.

Friday

CHAPTER TWO

Hate

Axel

That memory was forever ingrained in my mind. With my dick still wet, I shoved it into my jeans and took off like a coward. The weight of everything combined hit me like an anvil in a cartoon and I did the only thing I knew how to do.

I ran.

Marie was important to me and deserved better, but I couldn't cope with what she said. Those were words I wasn't ready for. Everything was moving too fast. I didn't think we were a fling but I didn't we were serious either. She knew how I felt about my father and my sister. I came from a line of people with serious emotional problems. I couldn't be the man she needed.

I would never be the man she needed.

9

Friday

A week had come and gone but I still didn't contact her. Every time I thought about it, I chickened out. What was I supposed to say? That I didn't love her? That I would never love her? Wouldn't that make it worse? Shouldn't I just leave it alone?

But saying nothing was just as bad.

Eventually, Marie would tell Francesca. And she would march over here and smack me upside the head. The sad part was, I wouldn't stop her. In fact, she should bring a huge bat with her.

Everything was so messed up.

I went to work every day and didn't really pay attention to what I was doing. I kept thinking about the last time I saw Marie. She was naked under the sheets, horrified by my departure.

I saw the heartbreak.

But I didn't know what else to do at the time. The English language didn't help me this time. In fact, it was obsolete. All I relied on was my ability to get the hell out of there as quickly as possible.

Ugh, I hated myself.

***

Hawke answered the phone. "What's up?"

"What are you doing?"

"Hello to you too."

"Answer the question."

"Just got off work. Why?"

"Can we meet at that bar we went to last time?"

"Hold on," he said. "Are you in the city?"

"Yeah."

"Shit, what happened?"

"Just meet me." I hung up and set my phone on the table. My beer sat in front of me but I hadn't taken a drink. The bubbles still floated to the top and the glass was covered in condensation. On any other day it would have looked irresistible. But today, it was my ticket to sit in the booth.

Hawke slid into the seat across from me twenty minutes later. "You have my attention, Axel. And my concern."

"I'm in some serious shit and I don't know what to do."

"Like, homicide shit?"

"No. Marie shit."

"Girl problems...okay."

"She and I were having sex last week and she told me she loved me."

Hawke stared at me blankly like he expected more.

Friday

"Did you hear me?"

"Yes. But what's your point?"

"She said she *loved* me." I slammed my fist on the wood. "What the hell was I supposed to say?"

"Are you telling me you didn't say it back?"

"No." I'd never said those words to a woman in my life.

"Then what happened? You just kept going...?"

"No. I got dressed and left."

"That's it?" he asked incredulously. "You didn't say something to her?"

"I just told her I had to go." Now that I was saying this story out loud, I realized how bad I looked.

"Are you joking?" Both of his eyebrows were pointed toward the ceiling.

"No."

"When did this happen?"

"A week ago."

"And you haven't said a word to her?"

I shook my head.

"Axel...are you an idiot?"

I shrugged.

He rubbed his temple and sighed. "Axel, this is bad...like really bad."

"I feel like shit."

"Imagine how she must feel."

I cringed.

"You need to talk to her. You've already waited too long and may have missed your chance. You need to make this right."

"How?"

"Go back and tell her you got scared for a second, but you love her too."

"Okay, I'll do—" I stopped when I realized what he said. "But I don't love her."

"Cut the shit. Yes, you do."

"I don't."

"Axel, now isn't the time to hide your cards. I know how you feel about her. I knew from the beginning."

"Look, I really care about her and I think she's amazing, but no, I don't love her."

"Bullshit."

"If I loved her, I would know."

"Maybe you're just in denial. Being in love isn't a bad thing."

"I never said it was. But I'm not there yet."

Hawke rubbed his temple again. "Axel, I know it's crazy but you have to embrace it. You love this woman. I can tell you that right now."

"I don't."

"Do you want to be with anyone else?"

I rolled my eyes. "That answer is irrelevant."

"No, it's not," he snapped. "Do you want to be with anyone else? Answer the question."

"No." I couldn't even picture myself with someone else.

"Do you think about her when you aren't with her?"

"Yes."

"How would you feel if she were with someone else?"

Absolutely sick. "I wouldn't like it…"

"You love her."

"Hawke, that's not what that means."

"It does."

I'd never been in love before so I might not recognize it if it were right in front of my face but I knew that wasn't how I felt. Marie was special to me, but that was as far as my feelings went.

"Whether you get the balls to go tell her or not, you need to talk to her. You can't just walk out on someone like that."

My nostrils flared and I wanted to choke him. "You're one to talk."

He took the hit without reacting. "Totally different. I didn't leave and then end it. I talked to her face-to-face and told her what was going on. I didn't act like a pussy—which is exactly what you're doing now."

"I'm not a pussy."

"A whole week has gone by and you haven't said anything to her."

"She hasn't said anything to me either."

He gave me an incredulous look. "What's she supposed to say? Is she supposed to call and ask why you didn't say it back? She's smart enough to figure it out on her own."

I knew I was just looking for excuses.

"If you don't talk to her soon, you're going to lose her."

"I already did lose her." How could we ever come back from what happened? I couldn't be with her if she felt that way, not when I didn't feel the same way back. Those emotions were too intense for me. She wanted to go to a place where I could never follow.

"What?" He narrowed his eyes on my face. "That was your way of breaking up with her?"

"No...but we can't move forward now."

"Why not?" he asked. "Just talk to her."

"I can't be with her if that's how she feels—period."

"But you feel the same way."

"Shut up. I don't."

He rolled his eyes. "Whatever, man. You're going to lose the best thing that ever happened to you just because you're stubborn and ignorant."

"Again, you're one to talk."

He looked away, his jaw clenched. "Not the same thing. We both know that."

"I don't see a difference."

He turned back to me, his eyes betraying his anger. "Then learn a lesson from someone who lost the one thing that he actually gives a damn about. I lost her, and I'm completely miserable now. I'll never be happy again. Sometimes moments of joy enter my life, but they're superficial and hollow. They disappear like the passing wind, and then it feels like it never happened at all. My existence is crippling, and every day I just wait for the pain to end— even though I know it never will."

Speechless, I just stared at him.

"Axel, get back to town and fix this. You don't want to end up like me."

If he really felt that way, why didn't he want her back? Why was he spending his nights with random women? Why was he living in a city different than the one she lived in? "Marie and I aren't like the two of you."

16

He shook his head. "That's what you think."

"Marie wants something serious and I can't give it to her. I just had dinner with her parents, Francesca made a comment about us getting married, and then she tells me she loves me...it's just too much. I'm not a family man kind of guy. I'll never be a good husband and father. I told her all of this already...but she didn't believe me."

"Because she knows you're wrong."

Then she doesn't know me well enough.

"Axel, I'm warning you. Make this right or regret it for the rest of your life."

I stared out the window.

"Seriously, take my advice."

"I have to let her go."

He shook his head. "At least talk to her about it. Don't go on pretending nothing happened. That's the worst thing you can do."

How could I face her and repeat those same words without saying them back? I didn't think I could.

Hawke gave up when he realized he wasn't getting anywhere. He grabbed my beer and drank half of it in a single gulp. Then he slammed it back down on the coaster and spilled a few drops. The look of disappointment he gave nearly killed me. "It's your funeral, man."

CHAPTER THREE

A Visitor

Axel

Someone started banging on my door. "You piece of shit, open this door!"

I knew who it was.

Francesca.

"Open this door or I'll break it down, I swear." She slammed both of her fists against the door again.

I didn't want to deal with her, not after getting an earful from Hawke the other day. But if I didn't face her she would keep pestering me until she got her airtime.

I opened the door and walked away. "What?"

She came in behind me and slammed the door. "What do you mean *what*?"

I sat on the couch and got comfortable.

Friday

"You screwed over my best friend. That's what."

I knew Marie would tell Francesca eventually. Actually, I assumed she would have done it sooner. "I didn't screw her over."

"You're such a coward. How dare you walk out on her like that?"

"I panicked and I didn't know what else to do."

"Fine," she said. "I guess I can understand that to a certain degree. But nearly two weeks have come and gone and you haven't even tried talking to her. She thinks you guys are broken up."

"Because we are broken up."

"And that's how you end things? Axel, you were with her for six months."

"No, I wasn't. It was like three."

"Whatever," she snapped. "That's how you end things? You just walk away and never look back?"

"Not in those words." I rested my forearms on my knees and leaned forward. "I don't know what else to do. I didn't realize how she felt until it was too late. Staying away from her is the best thing I can do for her."

"Yes, you did know how she felt, Axel."

I stared at the ground and avoided her look.

"Because I knew how she felt about you. I saw it written all over her face. And you know what? I see that same look written all over yours."

First Hawke and now her.

"I get that you're scared of how you feel. We've all been there. But this behavior is unacceptable."

"I don't like it any more than you do."

"Then go talk to her."

I wasn't sure if I was ready for that. I hated myself too much.

Francesca knew she wasn't going to get anywhere with me. "Pull your head out of your ass before it's too late, Axel." She walked out and slammed the door as hard as she could.

I continued to sit there, feeling alone.

Friday

CHAPTER FOUR

Two Weeks

Marie

It'd been two weeks since I'd seen Axel. The time had come and gone quickly, but in my mind, it felt like an eternity. My phone never lit up with a text message or phone call from him. Now it was beginning to feel like he'd never been around at all.

I clocked out then headed home, driving slower than usual. There was no longer any excitement in my life and I wasn't eager to go anywhere. Normally, I'd rush home and shower because I was anxious to see Axel. But now I knew there was no one to get dressed up for.

When I pulled into my driveway, I saw Axel's truck against the curb.

My heart jumped into my throat and I could barely breathe. I couldn't believe he was there, waiting for me to come home from work.

Deep in my heart, I hoped he was there to work things out. I hoped he would apologize for his stupidity, tell me he loved me, and then ask me to be with him again.

I knew I would say yes.

But what if he was there to say something else? To end the relationship that was already dead? What would I do then?

I took a deep breath before I got out of the car. I shouldered my purse like always and carried myself with as much respect as possible. After seeing Francesca spiral out of control, I realized I never wanted anyone to see me like that—pathetically weak. I held my head high as I walked to his truck, keeping a stoic face and pretending I didn't have a care in the world.

He got out of the driver's side then came around the front, his hands in the pockets of his jeans. He stared at me with eyes mixed with sorrow and guilt. I was surprised he could look me in the eye at all. "You've got a minute?"

I already knew what kind of conversation this was going to be. My heart broke all over again but I kept that pain bottled deep inside. I refused to give him the satisfaction of hurting me. "Only a minute. I have somewhere to be." I stared at him head-on and kept my voice steady.

He didn't ask what kind of plans I had. "I'm sorry about the way I left...it was wrong."

It was completely wrong.

"I panicked and didn't think. I just ran. It wasn't fair to you."

No, it wasn't.

"I didn't mean to hurt you. I wasn't ready to hear those words, and when I did, I didn't handle it well."

"It's okay, Axel. It seems like a lifetime ago now." I kept my cool but died inside. I already told him I loved him, so I wasn't sure how well I could play this off. Could I really convince him of indifference if I just told him I loved him two weeks ago?

"I feel like shit." His voice cracked, like he meant every word. "I loved being in this relationship and I really care about you but...I don't feel the same way."

Ouch.

Unbearable pain.

It hurts.

Make it stop.

"And I'll never feel the same way," he continued. "I just...I'm not that kind of person. After what happened with my parents and Francesca I just can't be that kind of man. I don't see myself ever getting married or having kids.

I never expected you to fall in love with me, so it was okay at the time, but now that I know you feel this way, I can't be here anymore."

His idiotic belief that there was something wrong with him was stupid. He was perfectly capable of being a great man. He had the potential to love endlessly. He looked after Francesca like a father. All these insecurities and doubts were stupid but I didn't waste my time telling him otherwise. He already made up his mind. "That's fine, Axel." I knew the second I walked into my bedroom I would burst into uncontrollable tears. But for now, I remained strong. "I get it."

"I'm sorry…for everything."

"It's okay. Life goes on." All I could do was be cold to him, just the way he was cold to me when he walked out of my bedroom. There was so much more I wanted to say, to tell him he let me down and broke my heart. I didn't trust him in the beginning because he seemed superficial and dangerous. That instinct turned out to be right. But he wasn't worth my time, and it would just make me seem bitter and angry.

He stared at me like he didn't know what else to say. He clearly expected this conversation to go differently, for me to have a more profound reaction.

Hell no.

I eyed the time on my phone. "I really need to shower and get ready. I'll see you around." I turned and walked down the path that led to the front door. As soon as I got inside I could fall apart and give into my grief. I just had a few more steps.

"Marie?"

I stopped and took a deep breath before I turned around. "What?" My voice stayed strong but it wouldn't last much longer.

"I really wish things were different..." He took a deep breath as he stared at me. Then without saying goodbye he got back into his truck and started the engine.

I walked inside the house and shut the door behind me as casually as possible, trying to make it seem like his presence and absence didn't affect me in the least. But as soon as the door was closed my bottom lip quivered and my eyes welled up with tears.

I darted into my room and shut the door, wanting to be alone with my own devastation. I hadn't given him the opportunity to see how much he hurt me, but now I got little satisfaction out of that. All I wanted to do was go to sleep and never wake up again. With my hands to my face, I sobbed. The tears dripped down my hands and forearms, and somehow I felt worse for getting so emotional.

A pair of warm arms wrapped around me, and Francesca's scent came into my nose. She guided my head into my lap where she stroked my hair and allowed me to cry. She hushed me and rubbed my back, doing everything she could to make me feel better. "Marie, I'm sorry..."

I tried to stop crying but I couldn't.

"You deserve better. And you'll find him someday."

I sniffed and stopped the tears for only an instant. "Would I be pathetic if I said I still wanted him...?"

Her hand paused in the middle of my back before it began to move again. "No. Not at all."

CHAPTER FIVE

Shipwrecked

Axel

"Axel."

I snapped out of my daydream when I heard my boss snap at me. I sat upright in my chair and stopped staring aimlessly at my computer screen. "Yes, sir?"

He tossed the folder onto my desk. "What the hell is this?"

"Sorry?" I grabbed the folder and opened it.

"Why are these reports over a week old?"

I flipped through the pages and realized he was right. They were old documents I intended to throw away. Somehow, they got slipped inside instead. "There must have been a mix up."

Friday

"A mix up?" he snapped. "I was just about to give this portfolio to the Petersons. You know, the owners of NAIL and STEEL. Do you realize how stupid we would have looked giving that to them?"

"You're right. It won't happen again."

"Damn right it won't. Get your shit together, Axel. You've been dead weight around here for over a week." He turned around and marched off while everyone else pretended they didn't overhear the argument in their cubicles.

I tossed the folder on my desk and closed my eyes, willing this nightmare just to end already. It was impossible for me to concentrate on anything. All I could think about was Marie. When I broke it off with her, it didn't seem like she even cared. She was so disgusted with me that she was already over me.

Now that she was gone I returned to my hollow existence. My bed was uncomfortable now that she wasn't in it anymore. I had no drive to succeed at work because I didn't have any purpose. My chest constantly thudded like it wasn't working properly.

I was miserable.

Breaking it off with her was the right decision despite how much it hurt.

At least I had to keep telling myself that.

Marie deserved to be with someone that could give her all the things she deserved. I hadn't realized she pictured me as a possible husband or father to her children. I hadn't realized she loved me.

I knew I adored her and thought the world of her. If something were to happen to her, I would die. I was fond of her in ways I couldn't explain. I'd take a bullet for her if it ever came down to it.

But there was no way I loved her.

I simply didn't have that kind of capacity, not after all the people I've lost and almost lost. I was damaged goods, whether I wanted to admit it or not. Marie was full of life and vigor. She deserved to be with someone who could love her completely, that would be there when the times got tough.

She didn't deserve a coward—like me.

"Damn, what's wrong with you?" Alexia came to my cubicle, wearing a ridiculously short skirt like usual.

"Bad day." *Bad month, actually.*

"I picked up on that."

"I'm just going through a hard time...can't concentrate."

"Girl trouble?" She leaned against my desk.

"You could say that." *Was I having girl trouble if I didn't have a girl at all?*

"What happened?"

"We broke up..." Saying the words out loud hurt. It hurt more than I expected it to.

"That's too bad." She didn't seem sincere at all. It didn't seem like she gave a damn, actually.

"Yeah."

"May I ask why?"

There was no simple answer I could give. "It just didn't work out..." Because I was too fucked up to be good to her.

"Sounds complicated."

"Yep." I turned back to my computer because I assumed the conversation was over. "Well, I should get back to work."

She didn't walk away. "Want to get a drink after work?" She crossed her legs, and her skirt moved up slightly, showing more thigh than necessary. She had nice legs, similar to Marie's.

I eyed her calves then looked away. I'd been with Alexia before and the sex was good. It was the carnal kind where your headboard crashed into the wall until it made a dent, not the slow and sensual kind I had with Marie. Getting laid might make me feel better and move on.

But I didn't want it. "Not tonight. Maybe some other time."

"Alright. I guess I'll drink alone..." She left my cubicle and sauntered away, shaking her hips purposely.

I turned back to the computer and tried to get back to work.

But all I could do was think about Marie.

***

I lay in bed and stared at the ceiling.

No matter how hard I tried I couldn't get to sleep. I just lay there, eyes ever open. My apartment was quiet—too quiet. And it started to smell. When Marie was a regular visitor she spruced up the place. Sometimes she would put scented candles in my bathroom, usually lavender scent. She would do the dishes in the sink even though I asked her not to. And she always washed my sheets and bedding every Friday, using her own detergent.

Basically, she made the place smell like her.

But now that scent had faded away. It started to smell like old gym clothes and dirty dishes.

Friday

My scent.

I hadn't gotten a good night's rest in nearly a month. The mattress was uncomfortable and the sheets were too thick. Every time I turned over my back ached. There wasn't a single position that felt right. Over and over, I turned one way and then another way.

Ugh.

I had no problem falling asleep at my desk at the office, probably because the distant sound of voices, phones, and fingers hitting the keyboard lulled me into sleep. But when I was alone, haunted by Marie's ghost, I couldn't find peace.

I missed her.

Like crazy.

Did she miss me? Did she ever think about me?

Did she hate me?

I turned over again then sighed when I realized I was more uncomfortable than I was a moment ago. Since I couldn't sleep anyway I got out of bed and headed to my truck.

It was one in the morning and there were no cars on the street. I started the engine then drove to Marie's house, unsure what the hell I was doing. I slowly crept up to the house and realized all the lights were off. After I parked at the curb I killed the engine.

I could see her window from here. She was lying in bed right that moment, snuggling with a pillow between her legs. She always slept that way, wanting to keep her knees apart. She probably slept in one of her old softball shirts. That's what she usually wore when she didn't have anything of mine to wear. Her hair was probably in a high ponytail and her fingernails were painted some bright color.

I wasn't lying beside her but I was as close as possible. Since I was so desperate to get some sleep I decided to sleep there. After a few moments my eyes closed and my heartbeat slowed.

And I finally fell asleep.

Friday

CHAPTER SIX

Being Single
Marie

Break-ups suck.

I didn't think Axel was going to be my husband but I didn't think we were going to end so soon either. Now I was back on the market trying to find someone new. But everywhere I looked I saw Axel.

Despite what he did to me, I still wanted him. I missed him.

And I still loved him.

"How long does it suck like this?" I sat across from Francesca at the kitchen table. I was painting my nails black to reflect my mood.

Francesca shrugged. "I couldn't tell you."

"How long did it take you to get over Hawke?"

She raised both eyebrows.

Friday

"Shit..." I forgot I wasn't supposed to mention him ever again. "Forget I asked."

She was flipping through a Martha Stewart magazine. "Who said I was over him?"

I stopped painting my nails and looked at her. "You aren't...?" She was still dating Cameron and it seemed to be going well. I assumed Hawke was a thing of the past.

"I'll never be over him, Marie. Not really."

When she said things like that it made me realize how tame my break up was in comparison. Axel's absence devastated me, but I never thought he was my soul mate. "Oh..."

"But I can tell you it gets easier...in time." She dog-eared a page then made some notes.

"Like, how long?"

"At least three months. Maybe more."

Three freaking months? Ugh. "Great..."

"Sorry. That's the truth."

"I wish I never dated him." My hand slipped and I smeared paint across the top of my fingers. I grabbed the rubbing alcohol and scrubbed it off. I took off the paint from my other nails and had to start over.

Francesca watched me with non-judgmental eyes.

"I wish we just slept together and that was it. I wish nothing else happened." I started over and added a fresh coat of paint.

Francesca kept staring at me. "For what it's worth, I think he loved you. Actually, I think he still loves you."

God, I wish that were true. "Frankie, he doesn't. He said it to my face."

"Yeah, I know what he said. But I also think he doesn't realize he loves you."

I rolled my eyes.

"Look, I know Axel better than you do—in a lot of ways. Sometimes he gets these weird thoughts and sometimes he doesn't understand how he feels about certain things. I think he's scared to fall in love because he can't handle losing someone else—because he's already lost so many people. Then he almost lost me...it's a defense mechanism. It's easier to let you go now than later."

"Did you learn that bullshit in psych?"

"Marie." Her voice turned heated. "I know what I'm talking about."

"I really don't think you do. He even went so far as to say he would never love me."

"Again, denial."

"Well, even if he is it doesn't help me." I blew on my nails so they would dry faster.

"Maybe some time apart will make him realize what he's lost. And he'll come back."

The idea of him getting on his hands and knees and begging me to take him back filled with me an unnatural level of joy. But it was a dream—not even close to reality. "I'm not going to sit around and wait for him."

"I didn't tell you to."

"Glad we understand each other." I was being hostile to Francesca when she didn't deserve it, but after all the shit she put me through, I was entitled to vent my anger to her.

"Do you want to go out on a date?"

"With you?" I stopped blowing my eyes and stared at her.

"I guess we could do that if you're interested. But I was referring to Jason. Remember, he asked you out at The Grind."

"Oh yeah..." I forgot about that.

"I can talk to Cameron about it."

I just said I wasn't going to wait around for Axel, but now that I was put on the spot I didn't know what to do. The idea of actually going out with someone, kissing someone, and even sleeping with someone made me sick.

Francesca caught my unease. "You don't have to decide right now. Give it some time."

"I just don't think I'm ready to date..."

E. L. Todd

"I understand."

I bet Axel was hitting the town just like he used to. The idea gave me such a bout of nausea that I had to swallow the vomit that crept into my throat. The idea of him being with someone else...was something I couldn't even contemplate.

***

"Do you want to go out with Cameron and me?" Francesca was ready for their date. She was dressed up in a skirt and a blouse, and her hair was done in pretty curls.

"And be the third wheel? No thanks." I shoved the popcorn into my mouth and changed the channel.

"You wouldn't be the third wheel." She marched in the living room and blocked my sight of the TV.

"Yes, I would. Don't worry about me. Go out and have a great time."

"How can I go out when my best friend is miserable?"

"I'm not miserable."

She looked me up and down like I was a pile of trash sitting on her couch.

"Okay, I don't look my best right now. But I'm not miserable."

"Just come out—"

41

Friday

Someone knocked on the door.

I waved. "Have fun."

She sighed then opened the front door. "Hey, Cam."

"Wow. You look great." He stepped inside the house.

"Thanks," she said.

"Ready to go?" he asked.

"Actually..."

I knew where she was going with that. "You better go and have a good time. I'm not getting off this couch for anything." I shoved another handful of popcorn into my mouth.

"Is she okay...?" Cameron tried to lower his voice so I wouldn't hear him.

"I'm great," I answered.

"Do you mind if we have dinner here tonight?" Francesca asked. "I'll cook."

"Hell no." I set my bowl of popcorn next to me and turned to her. "Go out now, missy."

"I'm not leaving you when you're like this." Francesca crossed her arms over her chest.

"Look, I'm fine." I looked like shit but I was fine.

Cameron put his hands in his pockets. "How about we just reschedule?"

"No." I pointed at him. "She needs to get laid more than I do."

Francesca's cheeks turned bright red.

Cameron shifted his weight and stared at the TV like he hadn't heard what I just said.

"We're having dinner here," Francesca said. "No matter how terrible her company is."

"Frankie, just go." How many times did I have to tell her?

"No. You were there for me when I couldn't even stand. To think I would do anything less for you is ridiculous." She grabbed Cameron's hand and pulled him into the kitchen. "Want to help me?"

"Sure."

They disappeared into the kitchen but their voices still carried.

"Um, what's going on with her?" he whispered.

"She and Axel broke up."

"Oh...bummer."

"Yeah. I was hoping it would work out too."

"Is there anything we can do for her?"

"Not really," she said. "We can just be here so she knows she's loved. She did it for me and it helped more than she realized."

After a long pause he said, "You're a good friend."

"She's not my friend. She's family."

***

We finished a game of Monopoly around midnight.

"Why do you always win?" I asked.

Francesca shrugged. "Not sure. I must be smarter than everyone."

"But not humbler than everyone," Cameron teased.

I tossed everything in the box. "I'm tired but I don't think I could fall asleep..." I hadn't been able to sleep for a long time. Sometimes I thought about crawling into Francesca's bed but now I wasn't sure if she was sleeping alone.

"You know what helps me?" Cameron asked.

"Hmm?" I asked. "Please don't say counting sheep."

He chuckled. "Watching a TV episode I've seen a hundred times. It'll bore you so much you'll be out like a light."

It was worth the shot. "I'll give it a try."

"I'm telling ya, it'll work." He helped organize the money before he put the lid on.

"I'm tired too," Francesca said. "But I always fall asleep the second my head hits the pillow."

"Lucky bitch," I muttered.

Francesca ignored the comment.

"Do you want me to go?" Cameron asked. "Or do you want me to stay...?"

Francesca tensed at the question like he'd never asked such a thing before.

I tried to pretend I wasn't listening by excusing myself from the table and grabbing my bowl of popcorn from the couch.

"Uh...I don't know." Francesca's voice came out weak, and a little frightened.

"Sorry, I didn't mean to put on any pressure," he said. "I was just curious." He rose from the table and shoved his phone into his pocket. "I should probably get home anyway. Got laundry and stuff."

"Uh, hold on a sec. Just give me a minute...wait right here." Francesca darted to me in the living room. "Help me."

"Help you what?"

"What do I do?"

I glanced at Cameron, who was standing near the door and looking at a picture on the wall. "I don't understand what you're asking."

"Should I invite him to spend the night?"

"Frankie, that's your call. Do whatever you want."

"But I don't know…"

"What don't you know about?" I kept my voice as a whisper so he wouldn't hear anything.

"It's just…is six months too soon to be with someone else?"

Hawke had been with women longer than that. "There's no time frame. It's really up to you."

She nibbled on her thumbnail.

"What do you want?"

"I don't know…"

"You either want to sleep with him or not."

"If I do, I'll think about Hawke the whole time."

"Isn't that the case no matter how long you wait?" I asked. "He'll be on your mind no matter what you do. But after a few times, you'll stop thinking about him. Just be honest with Cameron about it."

"I guess…"

"You don't have to sleep with him. You can just fool around. You know, round the bases. Have you guys done that?"

She shook her head.

"Just kissed?"

She nodded.

"Just keep it tame. One step at a time."

"I guess I can do that."

"And if you end up wanting to sleep with him, go for it. You have every right to. And you like him, right?"

"I do."

"Then go with the flow."

"Alright." She continued to stand there.

"Now go back and talk to him."

"Oh right." She turned on her heel and headed back to him. "Yes, I want you to stay over."

"Yeah?" A smile stretched his face. "Cool."

Frankie walked down the hall with Cameron behind her. They went into her bedroom then shut the door.

Since they already went to bed I decided to close up the house. I was happy Francesca was getting back on the horse with a good guy, but I had to admit I was jealous. Tonight, she'd have a man to sleep with.

All I would have was my pillow.

Friday

CHAPTER SEVEN

Weakness

Axel

I sat in my car in the parking lot for nearly an hour.

I kept eyeing the coffee shop, seeing Marie walk around behind the counter. She wore one of those aprons that tied around her waist, and she was wearing cargo shorts that highlighted her long legs. Even in a work uniform she looked cute.

I'd been coming by every day in the hope I might spot her. Her work schedule was never the same. Some weeks she worked at night, and sometimes she worked in the morning. So if I walked in there right now it would look like a total coincidence.

And I could talk to her.

But I stayed in my truck like a pussy.

Friday

Why was I there at all? What good could come from this?

All I knew was I missed her. I wanted to see her, even if it was for just a few minutes. I was going to run into her eventually. Why not today?

I finally found my courage to leave my truck. I made sure my collared shirt was tucked into my slacks and my hair was on point. I straightened my tie then walked inside as casually as possible, like I didn't expect to see her there.

I opened the door and walked in, noting how dead it was. No one seemed to be in here when I got off work, and I wondered how the place stayed in business. Maybe a ton of guys came in just to check out Marie.

The bell rang overhead and Marie immediately approached the register on cue. She hadn't looked up yet because she had to wipe the coffee beans off the counter first. "I can help you whenever you're ready." She wiped her hands on her apron then finally looked up.

Damn, I forgot how beautiful she was.

Surprise fell over her face when she saw me. She almost couldn't believe she was looking at me. Her lips slightly parted and her eyes were wide. Her hair was in thick curls around her face, making her look like a princess. Her makeup was heavy today, making her look like a supermodel. Instantly, she recovered from the shock and softened her features, suddenly appearing indifferent.

It hurt.

I walked to the counter, and the second we were close to one another, I smelled her perfume. The scent immediately brought back old memories, nights when I made love to her in my bed. She smelled like the candles she once placed in my bathroom. A few strands fell down her chest even though she tried to keep it behind her shoulders. I'd never forget the way they felt in my grasp.

Now that I was there, I didn't know what to do. I was stunned by her beauty, like I'd never truly appreciated it before. All I wanted was to hop over that counter and kiss her—hard. She wasn't mine anymore, but on a certain level I still considered her to be.

God, I missed her.

Now I had to remember why the counter separated us. She told me she loved me and I didn't feel the same way. We wanted two different things. There was no other way.

She stared at me patiently, waiting for me to order something.

Friday

It occurred to me than that neither one of us had spoken to one another. We just stared at each other silently, trying to hide our thoughts from one another. "Hi..."

"Hi..."

It was like old times.

"What are you going to have?" The iPad was positioned in front of her.

That's right. I was supposed to order something. "I'll have a London Fog, please."

She tapped her fingers against the screen. "Anything else?"

You. "No."

"$2.65."

I pushed the cash toward her.

She took it and made change at lightning speed. Then she shoved it across the counter toward me like it was tainted. "Coming right up." She turned around and prepared the drink, moving back and forth between the machines.

I watched her, treasuring the sight as long as possible.

After she added the steamed milk she set it on the counter. "Your London fog is ready."

I grabbed it and placed a lid on top. "Thanks."

She turned around and started cleaning the machine.

I stood there like something might happen, that she might say something to me to make me feel less alone. But she never did. "How are you?" I just wanted to talk to her. Ever since she left, I felt like I lost my best friend.

"Great. You?"

"I've been better..."

"Francesca and I just tried that new Japanese place. It was pretty good."

"Cool. I've been meaning to go there." I hadn't taken a sip of my drink.

"Well, have a good one." She walked into the back and disappeared behind the curtain.

I suspected she wouldn't come back until that bell rang over the door, telling her I had walked out or a new customer walked in. I stared at my drink and walked to the garbage can near the door. I didn't even like tea so I wasn't sure why I ordered it.

I tossed it and walked out.

Friday

CHAPTER EIGHT

Messages

Axel

"What?" Francesca pulled the pan out of the oven and dropped it on the stove. "Axel came to The Grind?"

I untied my apron and set it over the back of the chair. "Yeah. He walked in and ordered a London fog."

"What did he say?"

"Hi."

"And what else?"

"That's it. We said hi to each other and that was pretty much it. Then he walked out." I knew The Grind was close to his office so he probably stopped by on the way home, not knowing whether I would be there or not. The next Starbucks was five miles away, and he wouldn't drive all the way there when The Grind was right down the street.

"Do you think he went there on purpose?"

"I don't know...I doubt it."

"Why?" She had powdered sugar on her black t-shirt and a little on her nose.

"If he wanted to see me he would have said a little more. He just grabbed his drink and left. I mean, we're going to have to see each other no matter what. Maybe he realized that and just got it over with."

"Or maybe he misses you..."

I wish. "It didn't seem like it."

"I stand by what I said before." She turned back to the pan and scooped the muffins out. "He loves you. He just needs to realize it. This time apart will pull his head out of his ass."

If that was his way of doing it, then I wasn't going to wait around. He stopped by The Grind, said two words, and then left. I could usually tell what Axel was thinking but in this regard I was blind. "How'd it go with Cameron last night?"

She placed the tray of muffins on the kitchen table and sat down. "It was alright."

"What did you guys do?"

"Fooled around. Kissing, touching, stuff like that."

"Third base?"

She nodded.

She didn't seem enthused about it. "Did you at least enjoy it…?"

"I did. But I kept thinking about him…" She grabbed a muffin and picked it apart but didn't take a single bite.

"It'll pass."

"It's just strange. He was the last guy I kissed…the last guy I'd been with. It's just weird to do all those things with someone else. When I was with Hawke, I thought he was the last man I'd ever be with. Having to date and try to find someone else…sucks."

Now that I was in the same boat I understood. "I know what you mean."

"Cameron is a really great guy," she said. "He understands what I'm going through and doesn't make me feel bad about it. I'm lucky I found someone who's willing to put up with me. But…I don't feel anything for him."

"Nothing?"

"I'm attracted to him and I like him—but I don't love him."

"Well, love is rare. It'll take a while for that to happen." The only man I'd ever loved was Axel. And it took me twenty something years to feel that way. I'd gone out with a lot of guys that gave me butterflies but those feelings were superficial. What I had with Axel was real. Would I ever feel that way for someone again?

"Marie, I don't think it's ever going to happen." She grabbed a muffin and slid it across the table toward me. "Try this and tell me what you think."

I stared at the muffin without processing what she said. "It will, Francesca. Just give it time."

She shook her head. "You don't get it. He was my soul mate. That kind of love only happens once in a lifetime."

Even after the cold way he left her she still felt that way? "You really believe that?"

"Yes." She said it without any hesitation.

"Are you sure you weren't just infatuated with him? Sometimes those feelings can be misconstrued."

"Marie, I know I sound crazy but I know how I feel. That's what we had."

I picked up the muffin and dropped the argument. "What's in these?"

"Orange and cranberry."

"They have these at Starbucks."

"But these are better," she said. "It's made with real orange peel. And the cranberries I use aren't dried out so they aren't as bitter and tart. Just give it a try."

I took a bite and slowly chewed. The flavors that entered my mouth were delicious but not overpowering. "Wow. These are good."

"I think they'll be a great addition to the shop."

"Everything you make is a great addition. Make sure you write down these recipes and put them in a fire-proof safe."

She chuckled. "I don't know if they're that good..."

Francesca had a real talent when it came to this sort of thing. "Have you thought more about the bakery?"

"Yeah. I still want to do it."

"Great." I was glad she had a goal in mind, one that she was so passionate about. "The semester is almost over so you should get started."

"I was thinking the same thing." She drummed her fingertips on the table. "I'm not sure how well a bakery would do here. We get a lot of tourists in the summer, but after that it's pretty dead. I need a place with a lot of foot traffic."

"Manhattan sounds like the obvious choice."

"Yeah, but the lease will be crazy high..."

"Go big or go home, right?"

"I have the money my parents left me but I only get to use half. The rest belongs to Axel, and I'm not sure if that will be enough. I guess I could apply for a loan and see how that goes...even though I have no collateral."

If there was one thing I learned about Axel during our time together, it was how selfless he was. He'd probably give all that money to Francesca if she asked. He wanted her to succeed more than himself. "We'll figure it out."

"What about you?" she asked. "How's the job search?"

After Axel and I broke up everything was put on hold. I had no motivation to do anything other than sit on my ass. "I kinda dropped the ball on that..."

"Well, let's pick up the ball again." She pushed the muffins aside and grabbed her laptop. "We'll find a few entry level positions and internships, and put your resume together. I'm pretty good at this sort of thing. I learned a lot in my business classes about what businesses want in a new applicant."

"You don't need to help me, Frankie. I can do it myself." Whenever I found the motivation.

"I don't mind, Marie. Besides, it'll be a lot more fun if we do it together." She gave me a smile before she waved me over. "Now come over here and let's start."

When I was there for her after Hawke left, I never expected anything in return. If I fell on hard times I knew she would be there for me, but I didn't expect this kind of comfort. She was taking my hand and guiding me, getting me through this hard time. "Thanks."

Friday

CHAPTER NINE

Aches and Pains

Axel

I walked out of the building and immediately loosened my tie. I had two job interviews back-to-back and I was relieved when the interrogations finally ended. Wearing a tie was the worst part. It felt like I was being choked the entire time no matter how loose the fit was.

I felt confident about my interviews but that didn't mean anything. There were probably twenty other applicants applying for the same job—and they probably all went to Stanford. I didn't go to a competitive school because I couldn't afford it, and that was seriously hurting my odds at the moment.

All I could do was hope for the best.

I met up with Hawke afterward.

Friday

"How'd it go?" He sat in the booth across from me and ordered a dark IPA.

"Eh." I shrugged then removed my jacket. "It seemed to go well but then who knows?"

"You'll find something. It might not be the job you want but it's your foot in the door."

"I guess." I'd always wanted to move to the big city but now that I might I wasn't sure if I was ready for it. It was a whole new world. Everywhere I turned there would be strange faces and places.

"Don't stress about it. It'll be fine."

I took a deep drink of my beer, needing my nerves to calm down.

"Did you talk to Marie?"

"I saw her a few days ago but we didn't really say much."

He gave me his typical glare. "I meant about your relationship."

"Well, I told her we were over and I would never love her. Honestly, it didn't seem like she cared that much."

"You actually said that to her? Are you an idiot?"

"It's the truth."

He rubbed the scruff along his jaw, irritated. "You're stupid, you know that?"

"Whatever."

"You're really going to let this woman slip through your fingers?"

"She already slipped, dude."

He shook his head. "You made the biggest mistake of your life."

I was pretty miserable.

"Now what?" he asked. "You're just sleeping around again?"

"No." I hadn't been with anyone else. Alexia was an easy lay but I didn't want her.

"And why not?"

I shrugged. "I don't know...just don't want to."

He rolled his eyes. "The truth is staring at you in the face but you don't see it."

"You're sleeping around but you claim to still love Francesca. So, what kind of point are you making?"

He scowled. "Not the same thing."

"Not any different," I countered.

"You can still be with Marie. It's not too late."

"You didn't see her face when I walked into the coffee shop. It was like I didn't exist. I didn't matter to her. She's over me."

"How could she be over you after she told you she loved you?" he asked. "She's obviously putting on a brave face. How do you not see that?"

"I don't know...Marie is pretty ruthless."

"Love doesn't just go away—at least not that quickly."

"I know what I saw."

"It doesn't hurt to try."

I shook my head. "This is the best thing for both of us." I stared into my glass and watched the foam slowly disappear from the surface.

"And you're happy with this arrangement?"

When I reflected on my life for the past month I realized I'd never been so miserable. "Not really. I haven't been able to sleep so I park in front of her house. Somehow, knowing she's somewhat close to me lulls me to sleep. I think about her all the time, especially at work. Everything is just different now that she's not in my life anymore. I went into The Grind just to see her because I missed her so much."

"And you still think you don't love her?" he asked sarcastically.

"I got attached to her. That doesn't mean I love her."

"Dude, you're the most irritating person I've ever met."

"Right back at ya." I didn't need to remind him of all the weird shit he had going on with Francesca.

"It's still not too late."

"Just drop it, man." I didn't want to talk about her anymore. Somehow, saying it out loud just made the aches and pains worse. Our break-up was permanent and we would never reconcile again. Someone else would sweep her off her feet and cherish her forever.

And I would be the loser who let her go.

Friday

CHAPTER TEN

Unexpected Guest
Marie

"I've got to get to work." Francesca tied the black apron around her waist and threw her hair in a ponytail. "I'll see you later."

"Alright." We just submitted my resume to a ton of different magazines in New York. A lot of them were unpaid internships. Hopefully, I would get a real job that could buy me food. Otherwise, I'd be living on the street for a year.

"Don't worry about it." Francesca could read my mind, like always. "Something will come along."

"How can you be so sure?"

She pulled her purse over one shoulder. "Everything always works out...in the end." She blew me a kiss before she walked out and drove away.

Friday

Now I was alone in the house with nothing to do. I had a load of laundry to take care of as well as a load of dishes but none of those things seemed appetizing. So I sat there and stared at the wall.

Whenever I was alone my thoughts drifted to Axel. I wondered what he was doing and whom he was with. That Alexia woman would sink her claws into him the second I was out of the picture. She was probably sharing his bed every single night.

The thought made me sick.

It'd been a month since we went our separate ways, and there was no possibility he kept it in his pants that entire time. He probably picked up different girls on the weekend and fucked them senseless on his bed—the bed I slept on. Now I was just a memory to him—if that.

When I saw him walk into that coffee shop I had a daydream that he was there for a reason—to tell me he made a mistake. The fantasy kept playing in my mind even though I wish it would stop. It would never come true and I needed to let that hope die.

Why did I ever fall for him?

The doorbell rang.

I'd been too busy thinking that I didn't notice the sound of approaching footsteps. I walked to the front door and looked through the peephole, expecting to see girl scouts or some pastor trying to convert me to a new religion.

But it was Hawke.

Wait...what?

Why was Hawke standing on the other side of my door?

Was he here to see Francesca?

Did he finally get his shit together?

I opened the door harder than I meant to and it crashed into the wall. The stopper wasn't enough to cushion the blow. Now there was a noticeable dent in the drywall.

Whoops.

Hawke saw the hole. "I can fix that."

The repair was negligible at the moment. "You just missed her." He pulled up to the house just three minutes too late. Now he'd have to wait six hours until her shift was over.

"I'm not here to see her."

"What?" All the hope inside me died. I thought he was here to win her back. I pictured the happiness on my friend's face, the disbelief that the love of her life came back.

"I'm here to see you."

71

"Why...?"

"Can I come in?"

I stepped aside.

He entered then shut the door behind him. "I waited until Francesca left. She won't be back for a while, right?"

"No."

"Okay." He examined the hole in the wall before he turned back to me. "I wanted to talk about Axel."

"Oh..." This was taking an unexpected turn.

"He's..." He ran his fingers through his hair as he tried to find the right words to say. "He's an idiot, Marie. I know how he feels about you. He says he doesn't love you, but I know he's full of it."

My heart pounded hard in my chest.

"He's confused. He thinks he's making the right decision but he's not. He's miserable without you."

He is? If I said I was happy about that would I be a terrible person?

"I've tried talking to him about it but he won't listen to me. I realized I had to come to you directly."

"And what am I supposed to do?"

"That I don't know..."

Well, that helps.

"Maybe you can talk to him. Confront him about it."

"Convince him that he loves me and should stay with me? Talk about every girl's dream come true..."

"I know it's not ideal and you deserve better, but it's better than the alternative."

"Which is...?"

"Going your separate ways."

I'd already been without him for a month and I hated it. Absolutely loathed it. "It's been a month, Hawke. If he hasn't changed his mind by now, he never will."

"You should hear him talk about you...he says some pretty serious stuff. He just told me he parks outside your house at night because that's the only way he can sleep...because he's close to you."

My jaw dropped.

"He told me he hasn't slept with anyone because he doesn't want to be with anyone else."

New life pumped into my heart.

"He said he's miserable without you. He can barely concentrate at work, and the reason he went to The Grind was because he just wanted to talk to you...because he misses you."

Friday

All of this was too good to be true.

"He can't say all those things but not be in love. It's just not possible."

I crossed my arms over my chest and tried to remain calm. Everything he said was music to my ears. Axel was suffering as much as I was. We couldn't stand to be apart from each other. What we had was more than just a short-term fling. "He really said that?"

He nodded. "I swear."

The blood rushed to my head and I felt a little lightheaded.

"Talk to him."

"And say what?"

"Tell him everything I told you. Talk some sense into him. Clearly, I can't."

After the way he hurt me, I wasn't sure if I could do it. I never considered myself to be a proud woman but I feared I had too much pride to do that. He should be crawling back to me, not the other way around.

"I know this isn't ideal. I wish he would just pull his head out of his ass. But I don't know what else to do. He's my best friend and I don't want him to end up like me. He deserves to be happy."

"End up like you?"

He shrugged. "Absolutely miserable."

I gave him a look of pity because even now I didn't understand his problem.

"I've done my part and meddled. The rest is up to you." He turned back to the wall. "You wouldn't happen to have any tools, would you?"

I shrugged. "Francesca has some stuff in the garage."

"Alright. I'll take care of that."

***

Francesca walked in and shut the front door. "I'm home."

"Welcome back." I hoped she wouldn't notice the wet Spackle on the wall. If she didn't look directly at it she probably wouldn't notice.

Francesca's voice faltered. "What's this?"

Damn.

"What?" I tried to play dumb.

"There's a hole in the wall. What did you do?"

"Oh that...it's nothing."

"And it's patched up."

"I accidentally opened the door too hard and I made a hole."

She came around the corner and set her purse on the table. "You must have opened the door really hard."

"Yeah...I saw a big dog outside and freaked."

"So...you open the door as fast as you can?"

That didn't make any sense, huh? "I just panicked." I turned back to the TV and hoped the conversation was over.

"Who patched it?"

She knew I wasn't the handyman around the house. I didn't know the difference between a screwdriver and a nail. "I did..."

"You fixed the hole?" She gave me an incredulous look like she didn't believe a word I said.

"Yeah...what's the big deal?"

"It's well done so I find it hard to believe a first-timer did it."

Why was she grilling me right now? "Fine. I called a handyman. Get off my back."

"Why did you lie?"

"I don't know...I thought you would get mad at me for wasting money."

"I'm not your mom, Marie."

"You're asking me a shit-ton of questions like one."

"Why didn't you just wait for me to come home?"

"It was my fault and I didn't want to burden you." Would this conversation just end already?

"You never burden me."

She should be a detective, I swear. "How was work?"

"It was okay." She set her apron on the chair and pulled her hair loose from the hair tie. She tilted her chin up and smelled the air, like there was a scent that registered on her palate.

"What...?"

"That smell..."

Shit.

"I know that smell..."

She recognized Hawke's smell that quickly? She could still detect it? He was here for thirty minutes, tops. "Yeah...the handyman wore too much cologne."

"It doesn't smell like cologne..."

This was going south. I couldn't tell her Hawke was here. She would fall apart all over again and have to start over. Things were going well with Cameron and she was doing better. All of that progress would go to shit if she knew he was here—even for five minutes. "Is Cameron coming over?"

She continued to sniff the air and ignored me. Her eyes glazed over her and her mind traveled somewhere else. Somehow, I knew exactly what she was thinking. She knew it was his scent. It brought back old memories, old kisses and caresses. She took a deep breath that was full of never-ending longing. "Will he always haunt me like this...?"

I'd never felt so much pain for another person. "No."

She gave me a look, her eyes coated with tears. "I wish I could believe you."

CHAPTER ELEVEN

It's Getting Late
Axel

I was going through a pile of laundry when I found one of her scarves.

It was a mixture of purple, green, and red. She wore it one night when she came over after a party. It was tucked into her jacket, making her bundled up and warm. It looked cute on her, bringing out the green color of her eyes.

I pulled her jacket off and began kissing her, feeling the coldness of her lips. I took everything off but left the scarf in place. It trailed down her body, hiding her nipples from view. She made a simple scarf erotic as hell.

I'd never forget that.

Now I still had it. I felt it in my fingertips, and without thinking twice about it, I brought it to my lips and smelled it. Her scent washed over me like a vivid memory. That kiss felt real, like it just happened all over again.

I bunched it up in my fingertips and felt the fabric, treasuring the fact it once belonged to her. I could use it as an excuse to see her, to return it to her. But I wasn't sure if I could part with it, a souvenir of what we had.

The doorbell rang and my thoughts were pulled away from my happy place. I stuffed the scarf into my nightstand then opened the front door, expecting to see a solicitor.

But it was Alexia.

"Hey, can I crash here tonight?"

"Uh…why?" We used to have a fling but we were never friends.

"My roommate has this guy over and he's creepy…" She shook her head like she was trying to shake off the encounter. "They're both ridiculously loud and gross. I'm going to tell her off tomorrow. I won't get anywhere tonight."

"You don't have any girlfriends?" I never asked her personal questions so I really had no idea.

"Not really."

That was sad. "Uh…I guess." I opened the door and allowed her to come inside. I didn't want her there but I couldn't be an ass either.

"The couch is all yours. I think I have an extra blanket somewhere."

"You aren't going to offer your bed?" she asked incredulously.

"No. Why would I?"

"Because it's the gentleman thing to do."

"Well, I didn't invite you over. You just showed up on my doorstep and didn't leave me any other choice. So, you bet your ass you're getting the couch." I opened the closet and grabbed an old blanket. "I'm taking a shower then going to bed." I tossed it at her before I walked away.

"Thanks…"

I ignored her smartass tone and kept walking. I wasn't in the mood to entertain. If she was there just to get laid then that wasn't going to happen either. My sex drive disappeared when Marie walked out of my life. I wasn't sure when it would come back.

Friday

CHAPTER TWELVE

Let Down

Marie

I stared at the door for ten minutes before I finally knocked.

I couldn't believe I was taking Hawke's advice. Axel already dumped me but now I was trying to convince him to be with me. It was the most pathetic thing in the world. It was a disgrace to all women. I was selling myself short and knew I shouldn't.

But I still wanted him.

The door opened but Axel wasn't on the other side. It was Alexia.

Alexia.

You've got to be kidding me.

It took her a moment to recognize me. Her eyes narrowed on my face and then a cold sneer stretched her lips. "And the ex appears..."

Axel told her we were broken up. And she was in his apartment. I could connect the dots.

"Can I help you with something?" She crossed her arms and leaned against the door panel, blocking me from coming inside.

I tried not to throw up. She was in his apartment and probably just finished rolling around in his bed. Hawke obviously misheard what Axel had said. Or Axel quickly got back on the horse as soon as he finished telling Hawke otherwise.

"Hello?" she said with attitude. "My boyfriend and I are busy right now."

"Boyfriend?" I blurted.

"Yes. *Boyfriend.* Do you need to get your ears checked?"

I was so close to knocking this bitch out. "Enjoying my leftovers?"

She shrugged. "One girl's trash is another girl's treasure, right?"

I couldn't believe this. When Hawke said all those things I actually had hope Axel did love me. But seeing this skank replace me so quickly disgusted me. If she was just a piece of tail that would be one thing, but to be in a relationship with her was another story.

It repulsed me.

She pulled away from the door and called into the hallway. "Babe, someone is here to see you."

Babe? What a fucking whore. "Just tell him I came by to drop off a few things. But if he really wants them he can pick them up from the house." It was the only excuse I could think of under such short notice.

Alexia turned back to the hallway. "Never mind, babe."

I didn't hear his response but maybe I missed it.

"Bye."

I didn't say bye back because I was too pissed. I wanted to rip her hair out of her skull then light if on fire. I thought I was pissed at Axel for moving on so quickly, but now I was more pissed at Alexia. She had skank written all over her. He really went from me to her? Maybe he never appreciated me when we were together.

Maybe I never mattered.

***

At the end of class I walked to the row where Jason was sitting. "Hey."

He looked up when he realized I was there. "Oh, hey. How'd you do on the exam?"

Friday

"Terrible like always. Want to go out tonight?"

"Uh…" He couldn't hide his surprise at my forwardness. "Hell yeah."

"Great. Pick me up at seven."

"Sure thing." I flipped my hair and walked out, proud of myself for getting a date that night. I wasn't going to let Axel ruin my life anymore. He hurt me more than anyone else I'd ever encountered but I was done with his taunts. I was going to get pulled under. I was going to hold my head high and move on.

I drove home then walked inside. The Spackle on the wall was dry and it was difficult to tell that a hole had ever been there. Hawke did a good job patching it up. I tossed my backpack on the table and saw Francesca in the kitchen. "I have a date tonight."

"A date?" She had just been squirting chocolate syrup directly into her mouth. She swallowed the mouthful then wiped the chocolate off her lips with the back of her forearm. "What? With who?"

"Jason—Cameron's friend."

"Oh…great." She held the Hershey bottle in her hands. "Um…I just thought you weren't in the dating place…just yet."

"Well, I am now." I never told her about Alexia. If I did, I'd have to explain why I was at Axel's in the first place, which would mean I'd have to tell her about Hawke. And I couldn't confront Axel about it either because then he might tell Francesca Hawke was involved...the whole thing was a damn nightmare.

"Are you sure?"

Just a few weeks ago I was crying my eyes out for Axel. But now those times were in the past. He wasn't hurting over me and I refused to hurt over him. I told him I loved him, and he grabbed his things and took off—right in the middle of sex.

Asshole.

"I'm absolutely sure."

"Okay..." Francesca twisted the cap until it was closed then returned it to the fridge. "Then I guess this is a good thing."

"It's a great thing. Jason will be here at seven."

"Cool." Francesca wasn't completely on board but she didn't object either. "Any phone calls or interviews?"

Not even a single one. "No..."

"Well, it hasn't been very long. Give it some more time."

Friday

That was my only option at this point. "I'm going to shower and get ready."

"Okay." She opened the fridge and grabbed the chocolate bottle again.

"What's gotten into you?"

"What?" She popped the top off. "I've just got a chocolate craving going on right now."

"Someone is starting..." I walked down the hall and headed into the bathroom.

"Shut the hell up."

I got into the bathroom and started the shower. I was in a particularly good mood, but I knew it was false. I was still numb from the pain, and high off the anger. I was so pissed at Axel that it blocked everything else out. Now I wanted cold vengeance. I wanted him to see how good I was without him—that I've never been better my entire life.

***

"You applied to *Vogue*?" Jason asked. "That's a pretty big deal."

"But I won't get it. Even if it were an unpaid internship I still wouldn't get it."

"I wouldn't sell yourself short." His plate was wiped clean because he devoured the entire thing. His second beer was almost finished too. We were having a pretty good time. He was nice and funny.

"I'm just being realistic. What are your plans after graduation?"

He shrugged. "Working for my dad's construction company."

"Then why did you get a degree in journalism?"

"I've always wanted to go to college even if I worked in a different field. Besides, going to school is better than working. I've been avoiding it as long as possible."

"If you don't like your job why don't you do something else?"

"I'm the only son so the company will be handed down to me. I don't have much of a choice."

"But you do..."

He shrugged again. "It's really important to my dad and I don't want to disappoint him."

Since he already made up his mind, I let it go. It was too deep of a conversation to have on the first date. "I get that."

"Do you want to live in New York?"

"Yes and no." I finished my chicken kabobs and moved on to the rice. "I want to go because my best friend is moving there. But I'm not sure how I'll acclimate to the craziness of the city."

"You'll do fine."

Friday

"Plus, I don't have much of a choice. All the writing gigs are in the city. Unless I want to write for a local newspaper or something."

"Good point," he said. "But I'm sure you'll love it. You can get Chinese food at three in the morning and the subway is always running. You'll never get any sleep."

"Well, I love sleep so I'm not sure how well that will work."

He chuckled. "You'll find a balance."

I finished eating and felt my dress tighten uncomfortably. "That was delicious."

He stared at me for a few seconds before he averted his gaze. "So...it didn't work out with that guy?"

I thought this might come up. "Yeah. We went our separate ways about a month ago."

"Sorry to hear that."

I shrugged. "It is what it is."

"May I ask what happened?"

"Uh..." It was an awkward story to tell. "I told him I loved him during sex and he took off."

Jason stared at me blankly, like he expected the rest of the joke to follow.

"Yeah..."

"Are you being serious?"

"Unfortunately."

E. L. Todd

"So...he just left? He put on his clothes and walked out?"

"In a nutshell."

"What a fucking douchebag."

"It wasn't his finest hour..."

"I get that it can be awkward if you aren't in the same place but to just pull out and walk away...is pretty shady."

"I wasn't too impressed either."

"Sounds like a loser."

I shrugged. "I probably shouldn't have said that but I wasn't thinking at the time."

"You shouldn't apologize for that. If that's how you feel you shouldn't feel bad for saying it."

Axel didn't agree. "What about you? Have any bad break up stories that might make me feel better?"

"Not really," he said. "I've never had a serious girlfriend. Women have come and gone but they aren't usually around for more than a few months."

"Any reason why?"

"I've never really felt that tug, you know? That feeling people always talk about when they find someone they want to spend all their time with. That type of sensation has never happened to me, unfortunately."

Friday

"It will. Give it time." Jason was a good-looking guy so he probably got a lot of offers. I was lucky to be sitting across from him.

"Thanks."

"I don't know about you, but I don't think I can eat another bite."

"Me neither," he said. "Actually...I'll probably be hungry in another hour. But whatever."

I chuckled. "It's from all those muscles."

He flexed his bicep for me. "You like that?"

"I do." I gave the muscle a gentle squeeze.

When the tab arrived he snatched it before I could. "Just to give you a heads up, I hate it when girls do the tab dance."

"Well, you aren't going to like me much then." I tried to take it from him. "At least let me pay for my half."

He put the cash inside and left it at the opposite end of the table where I couldn't reach it. "This is a date. My ladies don't pay for their food."

"Your ladies?"

"You know what I mean."

I didn't bother trying to argue. He clearly already made up his mind. "Well, thank you."

"Sure thing. Ready to go?"

"Yeah."

***

He walked me to my door. "So, I had a great time tonight."

"Me too."

"Can I take you out again?"

"If you let me pay." I stopped in front of the door and faced him, trying not to think about Axel and what he was doing with that skank, Alexia.

"Not gonna happen."

"What's with the old-fashioned crap?" I asked. "This is the twenty-first century."

"Some things never change." He put his hands in the pockets of his jeans. "How about Friday? You're free?"

"As a bird."

"Great. Let's do something then." He leaned in and pressed a kiss to my lips. It was a closed mouth kiss but still had a lot of potential. He let the kiss linger for several seconds before he pulled away.

I felt the attraction in the kiss and knew we had potential. But I also compared it to the kisses I used to share with Axel. Those always made me burn so hot I actually felt cold.

But I had to stop thinking about that.

"I'll see you then," he said.

I walked inside the house and tossed my purse on the table.

"How'd it go?" Francesca jumped from the couch when she knew I was home.

"Good. He's nice."

"So, you like him?"

"Yeah. He's cute and sweet...what more could I want?"

"Did you kiss him?"

"Yep."

"Wow..." Francesca stared at me in disbelief. "Are you really over Axel?"

It was hard to picture such a thing being possible but I knew I was on the right track. "I'm getting there."

CHAPTER THIRTEEN

Life In Passing
Axel

Was this normal?

It'd been five weeks since Marie and I broke up and I was still as miserable as I was the first day we were apart. Not a single thing had changed. I still opened my drawer and stared at her scarf when the sadness overtook me. I still parked outside her house at night when I couldn't sleep. When I was at work I kept thinking about her.

Was there something wrong with me?

I'd gone five weeks without getting laid, and that was a personal record for me. The last time I had a dry spell like that I was in high school. In this instance, I had no problem getting action.

I just didn't want any.

Friday

I hadn't stopped by the house to check on Francesca in a long time, and I thought it would be a legitimate excuse to pop in and see Marie. Maybe if we could be friends I wouldn't feel this way. Maybe I just missed her companionship and her presence. It was extreme talking to every day and then going cold turkey. Maybe that's what the problem was.

They probably already had groceries but I stopped by the store anyway. I got some baking stuff for Francesca as well as frozen corn dogs for Marie. I knew she loved those.

I knocked on the door before I used my key to get the door open. Francesca never gave me a key, but when she spiraled out of control, I took her spare and started to come and go whenever I pleased. "It's me." I walked into the kitchen and set the bags down. My heart was beating hard in my chest and I felt a little sick. Pretending everything was perfectly normal was a lot more difficult than I realized.

Marie was sitting on the couch beside Francesca. She didn't even look up when I walked inside.

"What are you doing here?" Francesca got off the couch and approached me near the table.

"I thought you might be running low. You're welcome, by the way."

She peeked inside and spotted all the baking stuff. "That's sweet of you but unnecessary. I'm making enough money to cover everything. You don't need to help out anymore."

"Okay. I just wasn't sure." I kept glancing at Marie, hoping she would acknowledge me.

Francesca pulled out the cupcake pan that was shaped like a strawberry. "This is actually pretty cool."

"Am I a good brother or what?"

"Eh." She shrugged then stocked the kitchen.

I wanted Francesca to leave so I could speak to Marie alone, but it didn't seem like she planned on going anywhere. "How are things with Cameron?"

"Good. I like him a lot." She placed the corndogs in the freezer. "Marie, he got the frozen corndogs you like."

"Great." She never sounded so bored.

Francesca closed the fridge then moved to the other cabinet.

I came closer to her and whispered in her ear. "Can you go to your room or something? I want to talk to her alone."

Friday

"Kicking me out of my own kitchen?" She rolled her eyes.

"I just brought you food."

"Whatever." She shut the cabinets then headed down the hallway. "Where did I put my phone?" Her footsteps disappeared then her bedroom door shut a moment later.

Now that we were alone, it was even more tense. The TV was still on but I knew she wasn't watching it. There was no way she didn't feel the tension in the room. Francesca was out of the picture and now it was just she and I.

I put my hands in my pockets and walked to the couch. "Hey."

Her knees were pulled to her chest, and a bottle of nail polish sat on the table beside her. A pillow was hugged to her chest and she looked comfortable. She wore Nike sweatpants, the kind that was tight on her waist but loose on her legs. She wore a razorback top that showed of her rounded shoulders. Her hair was in loose curls around her face.

She looked beautiful, like always.

After nearly a minute of silence had passed, she responded. "Hey."

Our typical awkward greeting was officially completed. "How are you?"

"Good. You?"

I was miserable. Utterly miserable. "All right."

She didn't look at me once.

Without being invited I took the seat beside her and rested my forearms on my knees. "I was hoping we could talk..."

"About?" She changed the channel but her eyes never pulled away from the screen.

"Us."

"What's there to say?"

I grabbed the remote and turned off the TV so she would finally look at me.

She turned her gaze on me, and the appearance wasn't friendly.

"I know this is hard on both of us. I've been going through a difficult time handling it—"

She laughed. "Yeah, okay."

"What?" *What did I say?*

"Nothing." She crossed her arms over her chest.

"Anyway...I've been lost. My world doesn't feel the way it used to. Everything is different...I don't want to lose you."

"What does that mean?"

"Francesca is my sister and she's your best friend. No matter what, we're going to cross paths. I just...I don't want us to avoid each other or be awkward around one another. I'd really like it if we could be friends."

"But we were never friends."

"Maybe we can start now." Not having her in my life at all was torture. I had no one to talk to or share my feelings with. I couldn't lose all of her. I needed some of her.

"I don't know..."

"What else are we going to do?" I asked. "I can't just disappear. Francesca is my family."

"I'm her family too."

"Exactly," I said. "So, can we make this work?"

"When you say friends...what does that mean exactly?"

I shrugged. "That you don't hate me."

For the first time, her eyes softened. "Axel, I don't hate you."

"Really?"

"No, of course not."

"Because it just seems like...I don't know."

"Well, it's uncomfortable. We didn't end on the best terms and it's hard to bounce back from that."

We didn't end on the best terms? When I broke it off she seemed fine with it. Unless she was referring to the way I stormed out of her bedroom with my shirt on backwards. "Would it help if I apologized?"

She looked away.

"Marie...I don't want it to be like this. When I came inside, you wouldn't even look at me. When I walked into that coffee shop, it seemed like I repulsed you."

"No...you never repulse me."

"I still care about you and want to be in your life—if you'll allow me."

Her arms relaxed and her hands met together in her lap. She stared at the black TV screen on the wall while her mind considered my offer. She bit her bottom lip gently, what she usually did when she was deep in thought.

If she wanted me to never show my face around here again, I wasn't sure what I would do.

"Okay."

I turned back to her, surprised by that answer. "Really?"

She nodded. "Us being at odds with each other can't be good for Francesca. I don't want her to get stuck in the middle of it. She's been doing a lot better but she's not completely herself just yet. We shouldn't give her any reason to stress out."

Friday

As selfish as it made me sound, that wasn't a concern. All I really cared about was seeing Marie, talking to her. I wanted to be in her life, even if it was at a distance. "You're right. It might make things difficult on her."

She extended her hand to me. "Friends?"

I eyed it and thought of the way she would trail her hands down my chest when we made love. I thought of the way she would cup my face and look deep into my eyes. I thought of the way she would rest her hand over my heart when I slept. I thought of all the things I could only cherish as a memory. "Friends." I grabbed her hand and shook it.

***

I knocked before I walked inside. "Yo. It's me."

"No one cares." Marie's teasing voice came from the kitchen.

Hearing that smile in her voice gave me a burst of happiness that I couldn't explain. "You're wrong about that." I held up the mail and tossed it on the table. "Since it was on the way..."

Marie grabbed the pile and searched it. "Bills...bills...late payment notice...bills...oh shit."

"What?" Francesca was still whisking the batter at the counter but she stopped when she heard Marie gasp.

"It's a letter from *Vogue*." Marie held the envelope in her fingertips. Then she held it out to me like she didn't know what else to do with it. "You read it."

"Me?"

"You're right." She took it back. "Wait, no." She held it out again. "I can't read it. What if it says I'm a stupid girl who needs to dig a hole just so I can die in it?"

"Uh...I doubt they would take time out of their lives to say that." *Unless they were psychopaths.*

"Marie, just open it," Francesca said. "I bet it's good news."

"Wait," I said. "Why would they mail a letter to your house? If you got an interview they would probably just call, right?" That wasn't the best thing to say but it was the truth.

"True..." Marie's face fell.

"Let's stop guessing and just open it." Francesca abandoned the batter and joined us, batter and flour smeared on her apron.

Friday

I held it out to Marie.

She shook her head.

"Are you sure?"

She nodded.

I ripped open the envelope and pulled out the letter. After scanning though the words I realized it was nothing good. It was full of disappointment and broken dreams.

Francesca could read my expression and already knew what the letter contained.

With every passing second the light in Marie's eyes went out. "They rejected me?"

I folded the letter and returned it to the envelope. "It just said they didn't have any more availability for the internship." I wish I could just lie and say something else. Marie was the best person for that job. They were stupid not to pick her. "I'm sorry..."

She released a heavy sigh. "It's my fault. I shouldn't have gotten my hopes up..."

"No." Francesca wrapped her arms around her. "They're just stupid, Marie. Don't listen to them."

"They probably picked some IV league students..."

I tossed the letter on the table and felt my heart ache.

"Something else will come along," Francesca said. "Don't worry about it."

"She's right," I said. "This is just one place you applied to."

Marie moved out of Francesca's embrace then slowly walked down the hall. She went into her bedroom and shut the door behind her, clearly wanting to be alone.

"Poor girl..." Francesca shook her head.

"They missed out." I couldn't personally attest to Marie's abilities but I knew she wanted that position more than anyone else who applied for it.

"She wanted this so much...I feel bad for her."

"She'll be alright. Something better will come along." She walked back to the counter and continued to whisk the batter.

My eyes were still glued down the hallway, thinking about Marie and her broken heart.

"Can you hand me that bag of chocolate chips?"

I heard her say something but I didn't catch what it was. I was too busy staring down the hallway at Marie's door. I wanted to go to her, comfort her in any way I knew how. She didn't deserve to be sad—for any reason.

Friday

"Axel?"

I walked down the hall then approached her bedroom door. The last time I walked inside she told me she loved me and I took off. Now it was hard to cross the threshold knowing that was the last memory we made together. My need to be there for her outweighed my shame and I stepped inside.

Marie sat on her bed with her teddy bear pulled to her chest. She looked like she was on the verge of tears but refused to let them out. Her teddy bear was bent at an odd angle because it was being squeezed so tightly.

I joined her on the bed but didn't touch her.

She stared at me without hiding her emotions. She wasn't just disappointed she didn't get the internship. She was devastated. "I know it's just a job...one that I wasn't even going to get paid for. But I really wanted it, you know?"

"Yeah, I do know."

She rested her chin on her teddy bear. "The worst part is, I don't know what I could have done better. I did everything to the best of my ability and it still wasn't enough."

"The problem wasn't you. They only had a few spots and hundreds of applications." My hand automatically went to her hair and I pulled the strands out of her face. The touch was automatic because I'd done it so many times.

She didn't pull away, like she wanted the affection to happen. "What if I don't get anything?"

"That won't happen."

"But what if it does?"

"You didn't apply to every single writing gig in the city. There's always an opportunity somewhere. Don't feel discouraged. You will find something. Even if it's not your dream job you'll work up to it. Where you start doesn't have to be the place where you end."

"I guess you're right..."

I moved closer to her on the bed and wrapped my arm around her. The second I held her that way I felt better. It felt so good to hold her the way I used to. That closeness and intimacy was something I once lived for. It was beautiful and comforting—to both of us.

I rested my chin on her head and closed my eyes, holding on to the moment as long as I could. Being right next to her was so much better than sleeping in my truck outside. Listening to her breathe, to those musical sighs, was the best lullaby I ever heard. "Baby, you're the smartest, most talented woman I've ever known. You will get something great—because you deserve it." I tightened her against my body and held her the same way she held that teddy bear.

Her face moved into my chest and she closed her eyes, allowing me to treasure her.

I held her that way for a long time because it felt like home. Feeling her in my arms was better than any other sensation I've ever felt. It was better than sex. I inhaled the scent of her perfume and wished that smell were still ingrained in my sheets. I knew I missed her, but I didn't realize just how much until that moment.

As the night deepened we didn't move. Francesca never came to the door to check on us. My eyes grew lidded and heavy, and when I peeked down to look at her face I noticed her eyes were closed too. She leaned on me like a crutch, the teddy bear slack in her arms.

I lay back and pulled her with me, placing her head on the pillow beside me. Her eyes opened to a sliver, and she looked at me. The sleepiness was still in her eyes but she registered my face. The teddy bear was placed aside and she automatically wrapped her arms around me instead.

I kicked off my shoes and pulled her flush against my body. We were both fully clothed and on top of the sheets but neither one of us were cold. I reached the lamp on her bedside and turned it off, blanketing us in darkness.

My hand slid up the back of her shirt and reached the small of her back. I loved resting it there. The curves of her body were appetizing but I didn't feel the hardness in my jeans. My heart was the one reacting, beating hard and providing my body with enough blood to appreciate this moment.

My hand left her back then dug into her hair. My fingertips grazed the soft strands, remembering passionate nights we spent together in this very bed. For that moment in time she was mine again. I closed my eyes and pressed my face to hers, feeling my body relax the way it used to. I was already drifting away, entering my dreams.

Because she was next to me.

Friday

CHAPTER FOURTEEN

Stupid

Marie

When I woke up that morning I felt refreshed, invigorated, and actually happy. I didn't get the internship with Vogue, the job that I wanted more than anything, but somehow I was okay with it.

Then I remembered why.

I opened my eyes and saw Axel next to me. He was wrapped around my body, keeping me warm and comfortable. His hand was anchored in my hair, his fingers glued to the strands. His features were relaxed, looking beautiful and breathtaking.

I missed this.

When he came into my room last night I didn't have the strength to keep him away. I wanted those strong hands to wrap around me, to give me the solace I craved most. I was weak and let my defenses fall down.

Now he was still there.

I wanted to keep still and enjoy his closeness for another moment. Having him there was a dream come true. I craved his touch. Even though he had a girlfriend I still wanted to keep him all to myself.

After I stared at his face for a few minutes, committing it to memory, I left the bed and started to get ready for class.

Axel stirred the moment he realized I was gone. He sat up in bed, his hair messy from the way I fingered it in the middle of the night. He wiped the sleep from his eyes before he focused his gaze on me.

"Morning." Having him sleep here was a bad idea. I was trying to get over him, trying to move on with a nice guy that wouldn't hurt me. Sleeping with him wasn't going to help me. In fact, it would only hurt.

"Morning." He ran his fingers through his hair and blinked a few times before he stood up. His jeans and shirt were wrinkled but he still made them look good.

"You should get going or you'll be late to work." I grabbed an outfit from my closet and laid it on the bed. I kept myself busy so I wouldn't fall back into his arms and beg him to never go.

"Shit." He looked at the time. "You're right." He pulled on his shoes then walked toward me. "How are you?"

"I'm fine." I just wanted him to leave. We didn't fool around but I still felt like we did something wrong. Would Alexia appreciate the fact Axel spent the night in my bed? I didn't like that skank, but I never wanted to be the other woman. "I'll keep applying to stuff and hope for something good."

He looked at me just the way he used to, like he wished he could fix all my problems for me. "It'll work out. You're destined for great things. I can tell."

I wish he would stay. When he said sweet things like that I wanted to fall back into bed and never leave. I wanted to make love slowly and gently just the way we used to. I wanted to tell him I loved him and hear him say it back. "You should get going…"

He glanced at the clock on my nightstand. "Now I'll definitely be late." But instead of leaving in a rush like he should he just stood there. He stared at me without blinking, looking at me like he never wanted to stop.

Friday

Heaviness filled the air and I felt the weight on my shoulders. I wanted to get back into bed and rip his clothes off. I wouldn't care about losing the internship if I had him in my life. Everything else would seem irrelevant.

The longer he stared at me the weaker I became. My resolve was slipping and soon I wouldn't be able to keep my hands to myself. Instead of waiting for him to leave I had to get out of there—fast. "I need to shower. You can let yourself out." I walked passed him and got into the bathroom. I shut the door as quickly as possible then locked it so he couldn't follow me. Right now I needed a heavy slab of wood to keep us apart. My hands had a mind of their own and they wanted to feel that powerful chest while he lay on top of me. My lips wanted his. My legs wanted to wrap around his hips and never let go.

I turned on the shower and made sure the water was cold. Right now I needed a splash of reality. These feelings needed to be bottled deep inside—so they could never escape.

***

The second I walked into The Grind Francesca swooped in.

"What happened last night?"

I clocked in and tied my apron around my waist. "Uh, hi."

She stomped her foot. "What happened last night? Did you get back together? Did he tell you he loved you? Please tell me he pulled his head out of his ass."

"Nothing happened."

She raised an eyebrow like she didn't believe me for a second. "So Axel was in there all night—in your bedroom—and nothing happened?"

"Yes."

She crossed her arms over her chest.

"He held me for a long time and tried to make me feel better...and then we lay down and fell asleep. That's it."

"No, there's a huge difference."

Difference?

"Did you just fall asleep? Or did you go to sleep together?"

"What the hell does it matter?"

"It does matter," she argued. "Hawke and I would lie together and hold each other, completely awake and aware of what we were doing. We would touch each other, feeling our pulse and our breaths. We would exist in the moment together, having an entire conversation in silence. We would do that until we eventually fell asleep. That's completely different than being so bored that you fell asleep without even realizing he was there. Now, which was it?"

It definitely wasn't the second one. "It doesn't matter. It'll never happen again."

"Marie, you better answer me."

"The first one..."

The bell rang over the door but neither one of us headed to the counter.

She didn't give me a triumphant look. "Marie, listen to me. I know what I'm talking about. Couples don't just do that sort of thing—unless they're in love."

"But—"

"When two people can sleep together and not have sex that means something serious is going on."

"Isn't it the opposite? When two people are in love they can't keep their hands off each other?"

"No. Definitely not."

Deep down inside, I knew what she meant.

"The relationship is more than just attraction and physical lust. It's about the relief you feel when he's just in the room. Your bodies need each other in order to exist peacefully.

That pull, that tug, transcends human understanding. Those supernatural experiences, the ones that don't make sense, are the ones that make the most sense. Do you understand?"

"No...and yes."

"Hawke and I had similar experiences. Listen to your heart and trust what it's saying."

I already knew exactly what my heart was saying. "Francesca, it doesn't matter. Maybe I feel that way, feel that tug, but he doesn't. If he did, he would be with me."

"But he does want to be with you."

I couldn't tell her about Alexia, not without dragging Hawke into it. I had to keep it to myself.

"He just hasn't realized it yet."

How could he spend the night with me and hold me then go back to his girlfriend the next day? It didn't make any sense to me. "We should get to work..."

"Think about what I said."

That's all I ever thought about.

***

I tried to sleep that night but couldn't find any peace. After sleeping in his arms last night it was impossible to get comfortable. I should have asked him to leave instead of letting him stay. Now I had to get used to sleeping alone all over again.

I tossed and turned then looked at the time.

2:15 A.M.

I may have to invest in sleeping pills—or get a boyfriend pillow.

I left the bedroom then walked into the kitchen. Eating late at night wasn't smart for my waistline but I didn't care at the moment. I opened the fridge and searched for something good. Most of the things inside required preparation, and I was just looking for an easy fix. I grabbed a slice of cheese and snacked on it like a mouse.

I sat at the kitchen table and looked out the window, and that's when I noticed Axel's truck at the curb.

I dropped the slice on the table.

Was it really him? I darted to the window and peeked through the blinds. It was dark outside but I could distinguish a few things. The front seat was reclined and I couldn't see him.

But he was there.

Hawke told me about this but I didn't believe him after I spotted Alexia at Axel's apartment. But his truck was outside—right in front of my eyes. I grabbed a sweater before I walked down the path to his truck.

Now that I was there, I didn't know what to do.

I peeked through the passenger window and spotted him in the driver's seat. He was fast asleep, wearing jeans and a sweater. His arms were crossed over his chest and he looked uncomfortable in the leather chair.

I stared at him for a few moments before I gently rapped my knuckles against the window. The sound didn't wake him so I kept knocking, lightly tapping my knuckles against the panel. I wanted to wake him but I didn't want to startle him.

Finally, his eyes opened and he turned his head toward the sound. When he saw me he flinched in terror, sitting up fast in reaction. His eyes narrowed on me, trying to determine if this was real or just a dream.

He pressed the unlock button on the center console and the door unlocked.

I got inside and shut the door behind me.

Axel wouldn't look at me, shame written all over his face. He adjusted the chair so he was sitting up. His hair was a mess and the sleep was in his eyes. Despite how tired he looked, it didn't seem like he got any true rest. "I can explain…"

I pulled my knees to my chest.

"Actually, I can't."

"Do you do this a lot…?"

"What?" he whispered.

"Sleep outside my house?"

He nodded. "More than I care to admit."

"Why?"

"Can't sleep. When I'm this close to you…it comforts me." He still wouldn't look at me, the embarrassment still in his features.

"I can't sleep either. It's been hard…"

"It's been six weeks since…you know. Why is this so difficult? Why do I still feel like this?" He rested his head against the glass. "Last night was the best night of sleep I've gotten in a long time. When I went to bed tonight I knew I wouldn't shut my eyes for even a moment. I don't get it."

"I know what you mean."

He took a deep breath and his vapor fogged the window. He closed his eyes for a moment, clearing his thoughts. Then he slowly turned to me, his face hardly visible in the limited light. "Can we be friends that sleep together? That's a thing, right?"

"Friends with benefits?"

"I guess...but not the kind that fool around. You know, we can sleep together and do stuff together, go out to eat and watch movies. We can just be friends that like to spend time together."

On the surface that sounded great. "Wouldn't we be right back where we were...?"

His eyes fell in sadness. "But it would be different. We wouldn't be in a relationship."

If we really did that then I would never get over him—not ever. Seeing him once in a while when he came to the house was tolerable. Even hanging out with him when he spent time with Francesca was okay. But anything more than that...was too difficult. "Axel, nothing has changed for me." I didn't want to say those words out loud but they were the truth. Six weeks had come and gone but my heart still felt the same way. I was still in love with this man, and now I feared I would always be in love with this man.

Axel looked away.

Deep in my heart, I hoped he would say the same thing. I hoped he would tell me he loved me and couldn't live without me. I hoped he would say Alexia didn't mean anything to him, that I was the only woman who ever mattered.

Friday

But I knew he wouldn't.

"I'm sorry." I knew what that really translated to. He didn't feel the same way and he never would.

Hearing that rejection twice in a row was crippling. To say you loved someone and to not hear it back was one of the worst feelings in the world. I kept misinterpreting his actions. When he held me, I always assumed it meant something. Maybe it didn't mean anything at all.

"I care about you in a way I've never cared for anyone before but—"

"You don't need to explain." I opened the door. "Really, it's fine." I felt the tears start deep in my chest. He hurt me once and I hated myself for letting it happen. But now I let him hurt me again.

"Marie..."

I hopped out of his truck and held the door open. "Go home, Axel." I gripped the handle before I shut it. "I don't want to see your truck out here anymore."

He bowed his head in shame, like I just took something precious away from him.

"Good night." I shut the door and walked back to the house, feeling my bottom lip quiver. Never in my life had I wanted something so much—but I couldn't have it. I already cried over him once and I refused to do it again. If a man hurt me so many times, he wasn't worth my pain. Somehow, I turned the pain off.

And my heart.

Friday

CHAPTER FIFTEEN

Solution

Axel

For twelve hours one night I was happy. *Happy.*

But then the next day it disappeared. Reality set in and I realized what was really going on. I was alone and miserable.

Marie caught me red-handed outside her house. Instead of making up a lie that wouldn't make any sense anyway I told her the truth. I could only sleep when I was close to her. Sitting at her curb was the closest I could reach her, and it was enough.

I knew I sounded like a crazy person.

It seemed like she understood what I meant because she felt the same way. But then she rejected my offer to be friends—special friends. And then she reminded me of the reason why we could never be together.

Friday

She still loved me.

Instead of bringing me joy those words only brought me pain. I couldn't return those feelings, and those feelings were the reason we weren't together. If she just saw me as a guy she was dating, someone she was fond of, we would be okay. But that wasn't how it was.

I couldn't drag her along and watch her get hurt in the end. I had to break it off before things got worse. But somehow, breaking things off seemed to hurt us both even more.

Why couldn't things be simpler?

***

I hit the court with a few friends, playing a few games of basketball. Sports was my favorite hobby. It distracted me from everything else going on in my life. Right now, it stopped me from thinking about one beautiful blonde.

"Good game." Tom gave me a high-five. His t-shirt was covered in sweat as well as his forehead.

"Good game." I grabbed my shirt and wiped my face with it.

"You alright, man? You're awfully quiet." He tucked the ball under his arm.

"I'm fine." *Not really.* I started thinking about Marie again. "How's Stacy?" Stacy was his fiancé. She lived in New York City but he was moving there after they got married.

"She's good. But works too much."

"What does she do again?" I could hardly remember names let alone occupations.

"She works for Prada. She's a marketing executive."

Whoa, what? "She works for Prada?"

"Yeah. Why?"

"That's a fashion company, right?" I only knew that because I'd dated girls with the purses, shoes, and glasses.

"Yeah." He raised both eyebrows. "I didn't realize you were into fashion."

"I'm not, asshole. My girlfriend—" Acid burned in my mouth. "My friend applied for an internship at *Vogue* but didn't get it. Do you think Stacy could get me a hook up?"

"I don't know," he said. "But I can ask."

"Dude, I would owe you big time."

"You already owe me big time," he said with a laugh. "You still owe me two-hundred bucks from that game."

"It's yours if you get me a meeting with her."

The corner of his mouth rose into a smile. "I'm guessing this friend of yours is cute."

"She is. But that's not the point."

"Sure. Whatever."

"Can you get me the meeting or not?"

"She's coming down on Friday to spend the weekend with me. How about then?"

"I'm free whenever she is." If I could get Marie something at the company it would make her the happiest girl on the planet.

"I'll talk to her."

***

"Thanks for meeting me." When she walked into the restaurant I stood up and hugged her.

"Of course. It's always nice to see you, Axel."

I didn't know Stacy that well but I always liked her. She was nice, not snooty like most pretty girls I knew, and she was good to Tom. "You too." I pulled out the chair for her before I sat across from her.

"Wow. When did you become a gentleman?"

"Who said I was?"

"You seem different...a girl have anything to do with that?"

There was no doubt Marie changed me—in a good way. "I do have a friend that I really care about..."

"Uh-huh." Her smile gave her away.

"She's actually the person I was hoping to discuss."

"Sure. Tell me about her." She adopted her professional mode and listened intently.

"She's graduating this year with honors and she's getting her bachelor's in journalism. She's a phenomenal writer and she's passionate about fashion. She'd be a perfect asset for Prada."

"And *Vogue* turned her down?"

"For an internship. She was devastated."

"Why?" She sipped her wine.

"I know she wants to work in fashion, and *Vogue* is a great place for that."

"Did she apply to Prada?"

I hated my answer. "No."

"Hmm…" She sipped her wine again, her thoughts closed off from me.

"Stacy, she's a hard worker, she's passionate, and she's loyal. If you gave her any opportunity, even fetching coffee, she would be so grateful. If you don't think she's a good fit, I understand. But please consider her." I couldn't walk away from this meeting empty handed. I had to get Marie something. If I had to see that devastated look on her face again I would die.

"Well…" She pressed her fingers against her bottom lip as she considered my words.

Friday

My eyes drifted around the restaurant, and that's when I spotted something I never anticipated seeing. Marie was there, but she wasn't alone. Some guy was with her. He had blonde hair and blue eyes, looking like an Abercrombie and Fitch model. He pulled out the chair for her before he took the seat across from her. Judging the way they spoke to each other, this wasn't their first date.

Fuck.

Stacy spoke. "Our internships are quite competitive. The only applicants we approve of are from IV league schools..."

She was on a date? With a pretty boy? How long had she been seeing him? Were they serious? The jealousy and pain rose deep inside me and I felt sick to my stomach. I hadn't been this hurt in a long time. It was a freakish nightmare that needed to end.

But then I realized I had no right to be upset.

She told me she loved me and I still left her. I told her we could only be friends and nothing more. Every time she reached out to me, I rejected her. I kept hurting her over and over. If I really got upset with her, I'd really be an asshole.

Like she felt my gaze on her, she turned my way. Her eyes bore into mine, and the panic rose deep inside. She stared at me in horror, realizing that I was seeing her with some other guy. But then her eyes drifted to Stacy before the sadness set in.

She quickly looked away and never turned back.

Shit. She thought I was on a date.

She was clearly seeing this guy but I didn't want her to think Stacy and I were involved. The last thing I wanted was for her to assume I was sleeping around when I'd been sleeping alone every night—usually in my truck. "Excuse me for just a second."

Stacy was talking but halted in mid-sentence. "Okay..."

I walked to Marie's table, feeling my heart swell to three times its size. My stomach clenched painfully and I felt sick. Getting close to her, and her date, was nauseating. I stopped at their table and suddenly forgot what to say.

Marie looked up at me, horrified of what I might say.

Her date stared at me in confusion, unsure if I were a manager or another employee.

My eyes were on Marie. "Hi..."

Friday

She held the menu in her fingertips, looking small. "Hi…"

"I just wanted you to know that I'm at a business meeting right now. I'm actually having an interview for another job." It was a lie, but it was better than her thinking I was on a date.

"Okay…" She glanced at her date before she looked at me again.

"She and I aren't romantically involved. I'm not on a date."

"Okay…"

"I just wanted you to know that…" The last woman who had been in my bed was Marie—and no one else. If we couldn't be together again the distinction didn't matter. But it mattered to me.

"Alright…" She stared at me awkwardly, like she didn't know what else to say.

"Well, have a good evening."

"You too…"

I extended my hand to her date. "I'm sorry. I forgot to introduce myself. I'm Axel."

He eyed it carefully before he took it. His eyes widened in recognition like he knew who I was. "Jason."

"It's nice to meet you."

"You too…"

"You're a lucky man." I meant every word. I wish I were sitting across from her at that very moment. I wish we could have a few drinks then make love in my bed. But I was going home alone tonight.

"I know." He pulled his hand away and grabbed his menu. "Have a good evening."

I gave Marie one final look before I walked back to my table, still feeling sick and dead inside. I plopped down into my chair across from Stacy and immediately downed my entire glass of wine.

Stacy stared at me with concern. "Are you alright?"

"Yeah...just have a headache."

"You're as pale as a ghost."

I loosened my tie slightly. "Just hot in here...what were you saying?"

Stacy kept staring at me. "Is that the girl you're talking about?" She glanced over her shoulder at Marie's table.

I nodded.

"She's on a date?"

I swallowed the lump in my throat. "Yeah."

Stacy could see the feelings written all over my face. "She means something to you."

Friday

"I care about her…" There was no shame in admitting that.

"Why are you doing this for a woman who's on a date with someone else?"

There were a million reasons why and not enough time to explain them all. "I just want her to be happy."

***

Now I was even more miserable than I was before.

Marie was dating some guy—and that guy wasn't me. Despite how pissed and jealous I was there wasn't a single thing I could do about it. I couldn't tell her how much it bothered me—that it actually killed me.

What kind of man would I be if I did?

My days were even more meaningless than before. I went to work then went home. I woke up the next day and did it all over again. Every minute and every hour blurred together like it had no meaning.

Marie and I hadn't spoken since I ran into her at the restaurant. I had important news to give her but I wasn't ready to see her. I kept thinking about that guy sitting across from her. He seemed like a nice guy—which made me hate him even more.

When a week had gone by I knew I couldn't procrastinate any longer. I had to face the music and rip off the bandage. After I got off work and showered I headed to the house and walked inside. Francesca and Marie were both sitting at the kitchen table painting their nails while their homework remained untouched. "It's me." I locked the door behind me.

Marie didn't react at all, so she must have spotted me approaching through the window. She continued to paint her forefinger with concentration.

"What brings you here?" Francesca waved her hand in the air to facilitate the drying.

"Wanted to see how you're doing." I took a seat at the table, leaving an open chair between Marie and I.

Francesca glanced between the two of us, noticing the tension that just emerged from nowhere. "Well, I'm doing great. Cameron is picking me up soon."

"Where are you guys going?"

"To the movies."

I eyed her nails. "Will he really be able to see your nails in the dark?"

"Shut up." She blew on them.

I turned to Marie, who still ignored me. "Hi..."

"Hey..." She decided to change it up a little.

Francesca watched us like we were a soap opera.

It was awkward not to mention the guy she was with. But it was awkward to also mention him. I didn't know what to do so I sat in silence.

Francesca continued to blow on her nails even though they were dry.

"Jason seems nice." I finally said it. It was out in the open, breaking the ice.

"He is," Marie said in agreement. "He's in my ethics class."

"You've been seeing him for a while?" *Did she sleep with him?*

"It was our second date."

So, there was a good chance they hadn't rounded the bases yet. Thank god. I wasn't sure if I could handle that. "Cool..."

"How'd your interview go?" she asked.

"Actually, it wasn't an interview," I explained. "She's my friend's fiancé."

"Okay..." She clearly didn't know where I was going with this.

"She works for Prada in New York. I talked to her about getting you an internship—"

"What?" Francesca forgot about her nails.

I ignored her and kept looking at Marie. "But there wasn't anything available."

Marie stopped painting her nails even though they were only halfway finished. The sadness kept into her features at my announcement. "Well…that was thoughtful of you to try. I appreciate it."

"The internships book up really quickly," I said. "They only take about five applicants."

Marie nodded in agreement.

"But I got you an interview for an editorial position." I waited for her reaction.

She dropped the nail polish on the table and spilled it across the surface. "What?" She didn't care about the mess and didn't bother cleaning it up. "Whoa…what did you just say?"

Seeing the happiness in her face made that terrible night worth it. I had to watch her have a date with some other guy and suffer in silence. But seeing that joy made it less unbearable. "Your interview is next Monday."

Friday

"Oh my god." She covered her face and got the nail polish on her cheeks. "You're serious?"

"Yes." I forgot about all my pain for a moment, just basking in her glory.

"Oh my fucking god." She jumped to her feet and knocked the chair over. "I can't believe this."

"I can't believe it either." Francesca grabbed a towel and threw it over the nail polish to soak up the paint.

Her fingers dug into her hair. "I can't believe you did that..."

I'd do anything for her. She didn't know that by now? "I just wanted to help..."

She slid onto my lap and wrapped her arms around my neck. "Thank you so much." She buried her face in my neck, transferring the paint to my cheeks. She probably got it on my clothes too but I didn't care.

My arms naturally wrapped around her, sitting at the area just above her hips. I closed my eyes and treasured her scent. It washed over me like a warm tide. Her hair tickled me slightly, touching me the way it used to. Feeling her on my lap was heaven.

I missed this.

Marie pulled away when she realized she'd been sitting on me for too long. "You didn't have to do that."

"I wanted to." *And I'd do it again.*

"Prada is amazing," she said. "I didn't bother applying because I thought it was pointless."

I wish I'd given Stacy that answer. "See? I told you something good would come around."

"Because of you."

I shrugged in modesty. "You deserve the best. I'm glad I knew someone who could help."

Francesca cleaned up the mess then handed Marie a fresh towel. "I'm excited for you and everything but you've got nail polish all over the place—including your face."

"Oh, thanks." Marie took the towel and walked into the bathroom.

Francesca threw away the towel soaked in nail polish. "Seriously, Axel?"

"What?" My eyes were still glued to the hallway, waiting for her to come back.

"You're going to sit there and tell me you don't love her?" She blocked my view, her hands on her hips and a pout on her lips.

"Frankie, not now."

"Not now?" she snapped. "Axel, what the hell are you doing? Marie isn't just some girl.

I've never seen you do anything selfless in my entire life, so this means something."

"I care about her."

She rolled her eyes then stomped her foot. "You. Love. Her."

I turned away and looked out the window, not wanting to listen to this anymore.

"Axel, I don't get it. Please help me understand."

"Marie is just a friend, okay? People can break up and be friends."

"You guys aren't broken up."

Then why was she seeing some guy?

"You guys are just dancing around each other. When she moves, you move. Maybe you guys are technically apart but your minds are still connected. Honestly, your relationship is hardly different than the one I had with Hawke."

I didn't agree with that at all. "That's a big jump. He took off and I still don't know why."

"And you broke up with Marie and I still don't know why."

"I told you why. Marie and I want different things. She deserves things I can't give her."

"Bullshit."

I was tired of arguing with my sister so I dropped it. "I should get going." I left the chair and headed to the door.

"You know what?"

I didn't turn around.

"You're a coward, Axel. The biggest coward I've ever met."

I stopped in my tracks. There was nothing more offensive she could possibly say to me. Our father took the easy way out and abandoned us. He was the real coward. To compare me to him was painfully insulting. "Excuse me?" I slowly turned around, feeling my arms shake.

"You're scared to love Marie because you're afraid you're going to lose her someday. It's easier just to let her go now before it gets too rough. That makes you a coward. Just live your life and appreciate everything. Don't think about the ending before it even begins."

"Shut up, Francesca."

"I will not shut up," she snapped. "We all lose each other one way or another. People die, Axel. It's the way life is. You can't stop living just because that happens. I know we've both lost a lot of people but that doesn't mean we need to stop loving people out of fear."

"You don't know what you're talking about." I turned back to the door.

"Hawke left me." The tears entered her voice. "He promised to be with me forever. He promised to spend his life with me. He was the one, the only person I ever wanted to end up with. But he left. He walked out on me and left. It hurt—bad. But I didn't stop living."

Now I was pissed. I turned around and grabbed the chair closest to me. I slammed it on the ground and snapped it in half. "You tried to kill yourself, Francesca. Or do you not remember that? Was it all just a blur because of all the pain medication you were on? Just because you apologized for it, it's water under the bridge? What the hell would I have done if I lost you? What the hell would I have done if you left? You're all I got left but you still tried to leave. Now who's a fucking coward?"

Francesca kept a straight face but her eyes coated with distant tears, showing the true emotion underneath.

"You have no idea what I've been through, Francesca. You have no idea what it was like to sit at your bedside and hope you would wake up. You have no idea what it's like to get that phone call. Don't sit there and judge me for whatever insecurities I have. It's your fault they exist at all." I turned away and tried to get out of there as quickly as possible.

Francesca followed me. "You know how to fix all of that? To erase all the pain you feel every single day? You want to know how to get rid of it? I'll tell you."

I opened the door and walked out.

She chased me, hot on my tail. "Love Marie and let her love you back. I promise you, it'll fix everything. She'll fill that void in your heart. She'll make you forget that you're missing something. She's the answer to all of your problems. Don't throw her away."

I reached my truck but didn't walk around it. I stood there, breathing hard and combating all the pain I felt deep inside.

When Francesca realized I wasn't going anywhere she lowered her voice. "Axel, come on. Don't be scared."

"I'm not scared."

"Then you're in denial."

I turned around and looked at her. "When Hawke left, you completely fell apart. And no offense, but you aren't the same person anymore. It broke you so much that you turned suicidal. You think I want to go through that?"

"You won't," she said. "Marie isn't going to leave."

"You don't know that."

"I do know that. I see you two together. I listen to Marie talk about you. I listen to you talk about her. It so similar to what I had with Hawke. I didn't believe in soul mates before he came along. Only when it looked me in the face did I start to believe."

"Marie isn't my soul mate," I snapped. I didn't believe in that destiny nonsense.

"Have you ever felt this way for someone before?"

"That answer is irrelevant."

"No, it's not. Axel, you're totally different with her. She's not just some girl."

"And if she were my soul mate we would have been together a long time ago."

'That's not true."

She was irritating the shit out of me. "Look, I don't believe in your stupid magic hocus pocus bullshit and I never will. Don't try to get me back together with Marie by filling my head with nonsense. Maybe that shit worked on Hawke but it won't work on me."

"Maybe you're just stubborn and need to chill out."

"And maybe you need to mind your own business." I walked around the truck so I could get away from her.

"Stop wasting time, Axel. She's going to end up with someone else if you keep this up."

"She should end up with someone else." I hopped into the truck and started the engine. My foot hit the gas hard and I spun out before I hit the street. I didn't realize how fast I was going until I ran a stop sign. Then I slowed down, knowing I was about to kill myself if I didn't calm down.

Friday

CHAPTER SIXTEEN

One Too Many
Marie

Jason drank his coffee while his eyes remained glued to my face. He watched me carefully, like he was searching for something that could only be found in my eyes. "You seem distracted today."

I heard Axel and Francesca argue the other night. It was impossible to tune out. I hoped the fight would have a good resolution, where he would ask me to be his forever. But he took off instead. "Got a lot on my mind."

"Such as?"

"Well...I got an interview with Prada."

"Wow," he said. "I didn't know you even applied."

"Well, Axel got it for me. He knows someone who works there."

"The same Axel we met at dinner?"

I nodded.

"The same Axel you're still hung up on?"

I didn't see the point in denying it. "Yeah."

"For a guy that ran out after you told him you loved him, he sure seems invested in your wellbeing."

"He's complicated..."

"It seems like he's just as into you as you're into him."

I wish that were the case. "He doesn't want anything serious."

"You're telling me this guy went out of his way to get you an interview out of the goodness of his heart?"

"I guess..."

"I think there's more to it."

"Maybe...maybe not."

He sipped his coffee again and continued to watch me. "I don't care if you still have feelings for the guy since you're honest about it, but if you guys are going to get back together I'd rather not waste my time."

He had every right to feel that way. "I still have feelings for him and I doubt I'll ever get over him. But we're definitely not getting back together."

"What makes you so sure?"

"He has a girlfriend." I hated saying that out loud. And I hated thinking of the woman he was with. When he saw me with Jason I thought he might flip out, but he didn't show any emotion whatsoever—because he was seeing someone else too.

"Really?" He tilted his head.

"Yeah."

"He won't be with you but he's with someone else?"

"This girl isn't the type who wants something serious..."

"Oh...I see what you mean."

"But I understand if you still see this as a waste of time. Who wants to date someone that's into another guy?" I knew I wouldn't stick around.

"It's not a waste of time. The fact you're honest about it is really attractive. People always lie about that sort of thing. They'll date someone just to get over someone else. The fact you don't lie about it is really refreshing."

My lips automatically rose into a smile. "Somehow, you made me seem cool and not a loser."

"You're definitely not a loser."

"Well...thanks."

Friday

"It took guts to tell a guy you loved him. And it took guts to still be friends with him after that awkward ending. I think you sell yourself short."

It was the first time I actually felt something more for Jason. He was a perfect guy and he was sitting right in front of me. A relationship with Axel would never blossom and I needed to move on. "You're really sweet."

"Eh. My friends just say I'm a pussy."

I chuckled then looked down into my coffee. "Definitely not a pussy."

He finished the rest of his coffee then broke down the cup until it was a ball on the table. "You want to go to a ball game or something?"

"Sure."

"I'll buy you a chili dog." He winked.

"Ooh...and I'll buy you a beer."

***

As soon as I came home I knew something was wrong. Francesca was sitting at the kitchen table but a lifeless look was in her eyes. Depression filled the atmosphere, and I was eerily reminded of those months when she'd barely take a bite of anything. Did Hawke stop by? Did he say something to her? "What's wrong?" I didn't want to go down that dark path again, the kind where I didn't know if Francesca would be at the end of it.

"Nothing." Francesca played with a strand of her long hair.

"Is it Cameron?"

"No." She fidgeted with it for a few more moments before she let it fall to her shoulder. "Tomorrow is the anniversary of my father's death..." She grabbed the strand of hair and began to fidget with it again.

"Oh..." I always forgot the exact dates. I knew they were just a few weeks apart. "I'm sorry."

"I always think I'm in a better place when it comes around, but when it does I realize how wrong I am. It'll never be the same without my parents. To this day, I still expect them to walk through the front door."

I took the seat across from her. Both of my parents were still alive, and I'd never lost anyone before. I couldn't begin to understand how that must feel. She only had Yaya and Axel left in the world. It was understandable to feel lonely. "I'm here. I can come to the cemetery with you."

"No, it's okay," she said quickly. "I want Axel to come, but he never will."

Friday

When Axel talked about his father, his voice was always full of bitterness. He hated the man but couldn't stop comparing himself to him. "He never has?"

She shook her head. "He didn't even come to the funeral."

Damn, that was bad.

"I'm okay going alone. That's not the problem. I just think Axel is causing himself more grief by staying angry. He needs to forgive our dad and let himself heal. Every time I tell him that, he tells me to shut up."

That sounded about right.

"I'd ask you to talk to him but I don't think it'll make a difference."

"Yeah..." I didn't want to stick my nose in his personal business, not after that argument he had with Frankie. "Maybe he just needs more time to move on."

"It's been seven years..."

"Everyone heals at different speeds."

"I guess." She pulled her hair in a quick ponytail then walked into the kitchen. "I'm going to bake something...that's the only thing that makes me feel better."

CHAPTER SEVENTEEN

Anniversary

Axel

I called in sick today.

I didn't care if it pissed off my boss or piled more work on someone else. It was one of those days where I just wanted to sit in the dark and be alone. The date didn't escape my notice.

On my mom's anniversary, I visited her grave and brought flowers. I always took time out of my life, no matter how busy I was, just to see her. Sometimes I ran into Francesca and sometimes I didn't. We always mourned differently—never together.

But I wasn't going to my father's grave.

I didn't go to his funeral and I hadn't visited him once. If he chose to leave voluntarily, then he didn't deserve my sympathy or compassion. We just lost our mom and he chose to follow her rather than look after the two kids he made with her. I could understand that kind of despair, but I couldn't understand that kind of cowardice.

I tried to keep my mind off of it by watching TV. I lay in my sweatpants and t-shirt, the same thing I slept in. My phone was somewhere in my room. I didn't want to have it on me because I knew Francesca would call me. She'd pester me to visit Dad, like every other year.

I wasn't going to do it.

I was just about to fall asleep when someone knocked on the door.

Irritation immediately swept through my body and I ground my teeth together. Francesca only called me. She never arrived at my doorstep like this. It ticked me off because she failed to understand my personal space.

I walked to the door and opened it. "You're crossing a line—"

Marie stood on my doorstep, holding a bouquet of flowers. She didn't seem surprised by my outburst, like she suspected I would assume she was Francesca. "Hi..."

"Hi..." I stared at her in disbelief, unsure if she was really there.

"I'm sorry to bother you...can I come in?"

Where were my manners? "Sure." I allowed her inside before I shut the door. "Sorry...I thought you were Francesca."

"It's okay. I understand." She set the flowers down on my table. Then she stared at me, keeping several feet in between us.

I was a mess, wearing the same clothes as yesterday. My hair was in disarray and I hadn't even brushed my teeth. "How'd you know I was home?"

She shrugged. "Lucky guess."

Francesca must have told her what today was. There was no other explanation. If she thought she could get to me through Marie she was stupid. "I called in sick today because I wasn't feeling well."

Marie didn't buy it. "Do you have any plans today?"

I shook my head.

"Well, I'm going to the cemetery if you'd like to join me."

It wasn't going to work. "I'm not going. But thanks for stopping by."

She didn't move to the door after I dismissed her. "Axel—"

"I know Frankie put you up to this. I've made my decision and I'm not going to change my mind. You should just go."

Friday

"I'm not going anywhere." She crossed her arms over her chest and stood her ground.

"You're welcome to lie around here, but I'm not leaving."

"Fine."

"Fine." I moved to the hallway. "I'm going to take a shower. Make yourself comfortable."

***

After I cleaned up, I walked back into the living room. Marie was sitting on one end of the couch, wearing a black dress with wedges. Her legs were crossed and she was watching TV. I left the daytime cartoons on.

"I'm a child. I know." I sat on the opposite end of the couch, keeping distance between us.

"That's not what I was thinking."

"Oh really?"

She shook her head. "I like cartoons too. I grew up on them, you know?"

I leaned back into the couch, feeling a little better now that I showered and brushed my teeth. "My favorite was transformers. Yours?"

"Tiny Toons." She smiled at the memory.

"Good choice."

She grabbed the remote and turned off the TV.

I knew what was coming.

"Please come with me."

"No."

"Axel—"

"I said no. He abandoned me—both of us."

"I know," she said gently.

"He didn't think twice about it. He shot himself in our kitchen, knowing I would come home from school and see it. What kind of sick freak does that?"

Her eyes fell in pity but she kept pressing on. "Even so—"

"He left us as orphans. He dropped us on Yaya, who just lost a daughter. He was a fucking asshole."

"I get it."

"I don't think you do. I was still numb from my mother's death and then I came home to his brains all over the walls. You think that image isn't forever ingrained in my mind? It doesn't matter how many years pass, I'll never forget it."

"Axel, he's your father."

"And I'm his son—but he turned his back on me. Now I'm going to do the same to him."

"If you keep harboring this anger you're just going to make yourself feel worse."

"Shut up."

Marie's eyes narrowed on my face, and she looked like she might slap me.

I realized how badly I fucked up. "I'm sorry...I shouldn't have said that."

"Damn right you shouldn't have."

"I take it back." I felt guilty as soon as I said those words. Marie didn't deserve to be treated that way. "You should just go...I'm not my best today."

"I'm not going anywhere—unless you come with me."

"Then we're watching a blank TV screen for the rest of the day."

"Fine." She turned back to the TV and fell silent.

I stared at the other wall.

Minutes of silence passed. She crossed her legs then uncrossed them.

"When we're depressed we do crazy things," she said. "If you'd gotten home earlier I'm sure he would have changed his mind. He was experiencing a lot of grief and he didn't know how to handle it. I'm not justifying his actions, but keep in mind he was going through a lot. He just lost his wife, and now he was a single father to two kids. It would terrify anyone."

"My mom wouldn't have left us. If she knew what he did she'd be so disappointed in him..."

"Women are different than men."

"What kind of excuse is that?" I snapped.

"Women are more emotional so they can handle it. Men are different in that way."

"Don't justify what he did. He was a coward and we both know it."

"Maybe he was."

I turned to her.

"Maybe he was a piece-of-shit father for abandoning the two of you. But you should still forgive him."

"I don't have to do anything." If he could take his own life so easily, then I could forget about him. "I'm not one to hold a grudge, but this is different. I would never leave our kids like that, even if you died—" I closed my eyes in anguish when I realized my stupidity. I said something I could never take back no matter how hard I tried, and now that echo would live on forever. Marie heard it, and I heard it a million times over. I was stuck in that moment forever, reliving it. I turned the other way so I wouldn't have to look at her anymore. I was humiliated beyond words, confessing feelings I wasn't even sure I had.

Friday

Marie didn't say anything. She was dead silent.

I stared at the wall again, feeling the tension rise. It was palpable and hot, burning my skin as it pressed against me. I'd give anything to have a redo, to fix what just happened.

Marie rose from the couch.

I saw her movements in my peripheral vision. She'd probably grab her flowers then leave. After what I said, she was probably fed up with me. I made her so uncomfortable that she wanted to walk out.

She slowly approached my side of the couch, her leg touching my knee. I felt her rub against me.

I kept staring at the wall, refusing to make eye contact with her. I was aware of her closeness, even the rate of her breathing. Her scent washed over me, hinting at vanilla and honey. My heart skipped a beat when she was close to me.

Marie placed her hands on either side of my head, grabbing the back of the couch. Then she straddled my hips and slid into my lap, her chest pressed to mine. Her forehead connected with mine.

My hands automatically ran up her thighs until I gripped her hips. Her dress rose up past her thighs, exposing most of her skin. Her pink panties could be seen but I didn't look at them.

My heart wouldn't slow down.

Her arms wrapped around my neck and she kept her face pressed to mine. The swell of her breasts rubbed against my chest, and I remembered the way they felt against my bare skin when we made love.

My entire body was on fire. Feeling her touch me, invade me, made everything burn. I felt uneasy, but I also felt better than I had in a long time. The aches and pains in my body seemed to disappear. All I felt was the syncing of our heartbeats and the match of our breaths.

I forgot what we were just talking about.

My hands glided to her back, feeling the steep curve there. I loved the curves of her body. It reminded me of the various hills in the Swiss Alps. They were deadly, but also beautiful.

Marie placed her fingers against my chin and tilted my chin up slightly, forcing my look on her. She stared into my eyes, the look on her face matching mine. Her fingers dug into my hair just the way they used to.

Friday

Feeling that connection with her chased away all the anger and pain. The bitterness evaporated like steam on a hot pan. All I felt was the peace she gave me. It wrapped around me like a warm blanket on a winter morning. It was the greatest sensation I'd ever known.

"Axel?"

When she said my name, my entire body tensed. It was on alert, ready to obey whatever command she gave. "Baby?"

"Come to the cemetery with me." She continued to look into my eyes, forcing me to obey with just a look.

I still didn't want to go, but I didn't want to deny her either. In that moment, she could get me to do anything. She hypnotized me with her spell, manipulating me with just her touch. She possessed the kind of magic that affected everyone around her. She tempted me with this affection, the feel of her warm skin under my fingertips. For a moment, it seemed like she was mine.

And that made me crumble.

"Axel?"

Helpless, I obeyed. "Okay."

***

I didn't even know where the grave was. Somehow, Marie did.

She held the flowers in one hand while she held mine with the other. She stopped when we reached the headstone. It was a slab of charcoal marble with his name etched into the stone. My name as well as Francesca's was written at the bottom, saying we were his legacy.

I stared at it and felt nothing.

Marie held the flowers out to me.

I eyed them for nearly a minute before I took them. A stone cup sat beside the tombstone, a place to insert the stems. I placed the flowers in the cup and arranged them so they looked nice. Then I stood back and stared at the grave again. My father's remains were directly underneath me.

But I still felt nothing.

Marie hooked her arm through mine.

When I visited my mom's grave, I always went alone. No one was around so I told her about my life, the things that were going on. I told her about Francesca and what she was up to. She couldn't hear me but I spoke anyway. Somehow, it made me feel better. It made it seem like she was still there with me.

But what did I do with my father?

Friday

Marie stood beside me in silence. She didn't pressure me to do anything. She was just there—comforting me.

Seeing his name in the stone brought back so many memories. I remembered how depressed he was when my mom was diagnosed. With every passing week he became worse. He was heartbroken before she was even gone. Despite how much I hated him, I knew one thing.

He really loved my mother.

"Tell me your fondest memory of him."

"Of my father?" I whispered.

"Yeah."

I searched my memory and thought of so many things. Before my mom got sick, we were close. We did a lot of stuff together. "We used to go fishing a lot. Francesca would come sometimes, but it was mainly just he and I. He taught me everything he knew. On my tenth birthday, he got me a new fishing pole. It was a real one—not those little boy ones. I thought that was the coolest thing."

Her fingers rested on my arm. "That's nice."

"There's other stuff too...but I remember that one the most."

"Thank you for sharing."

I stared at the grass below my feet, noting how thick and long it was. It was lush and green. The graveyard was beautiful. Both of my parents were buried in a nice place. "I try to look after Francesca as much as I can but it's hard sometimes...I'm not sure how you tolerated her for so long." The words left my lips on their own. I didn't even realize what I was doing until it was already done. "I protect her and chase the dogs away but I don't like it. It's hard work. You know how she is..."

Marie rubbed my arm gently.

"I understand why you did what you did...but that doesn't make it right. Francesca and I always feel alone even though we have each other. It's just not the same...not having a parent." I felt my eyes water so I closed them so they would stop. "You should have gotten help. You should have talked to someone. You should have done something..."

My chest hurt from all the pain I suppressed over the years. "I miss you."

Marie rested her head on my shoulder, and her quiet tears echoed in my ear.

"I think you'd be proud of me. I think you would like the man I've become. But I'll never know...because you left."

Marie sniffed.

Friday

"I know I should let it go. I know I should forgive you. But it's hard..."

Marie tightened her hold on me.

"I'm sorry for not coming to your funeral. I'm sorry for not visiting. It was just too hard. I think it was easier to be angry than to admit how hurt I am that you're gone. I didn't know what else to do...so I started to hate you instead.

"But I don't hate you. I hate myself for not seeing the signs, for not doing something about it before it was too late. Maybe if I had, we'd still be a family right now. You might have come to my college graduation. And you might come to Francesca's." I stopped talking because it was becoming too difficult. I wasn't the most emotional guy in the world. Feelings didn't come to me easily, and when they did, I hardly acknowledged them. And I never cried. The fact I was about to made me tense in anxiety. I fell silent and allowed the agony to pass, to circulate through my body and disappear.

The sound of crunching leaves emerged from the left. The footsteps seemed light, like a small person was approaching us.

I turned to see my sister standing there, her hand full of flowers. She stared at me like she'd never seen me before. It was the first time she really looked at me. Pride and sadness came over her face, unable to believe I was really there—with her.

She walked up to me, the flowers still in her hands. Her eyes welled with tears and fell freely down her face. Her eyes and cheeks didn't turn red. All they did was moisten.

Marie stepped away, giving the two of us some privacy.

Francesca moved into my chest and wrapped her arms around me, holding me tightly. Once she was there she began to cry. Her tears soaked my chest, and her small body convulsed with the pain.

I held her and felt my own tears emerge, feeling the same pain at the same time. My chin rested on her head and I mourned for everything we lost. It was just she and I against the world. No matter how bad things became, we still had each other. It didn't matter how much we fought or how much we hated each other at times. The love we had for each other was unconditional. We would make it through—like always.

***

When we walked back into my apartment, there was only one thing I wanted.

Marie.

Friday

I didn't want sex. I didn't want to get off. I didn't want something physical and meaningless.

I wanted her.

When we were together, we always made something beautiful. When I was inside her, I felt whole. As our bodies moved together the pain was shaved off. We fell into each other, finding comfort the only way we knew how.

She wasn't my drug.

She was my cure.

Once the door was shut and we were alone, I went for it. My hands dug into her hair forcefully and I positioned her against the wall. I rubbed my nose against hers before I placed a kiss on her lips.

Her kiss was full of hesitance, as if the moment didn't feel right. She didn't kiss me the way she used to. There was more fear than anything else.

I pressed my body against hers and slowed down the kiss. I felt her lips with mine, sucking the bottom one before lightly caressing the top. Her lips were soft just the way they used to be. I missed this. I missed kissing her, touching her, and adoring her.

She responded to me, her lips parting and allowing me inside. Now that my body was open like a dam, everything came flooding out. I needed her more than ever, to fix this unbearable pain. I never felt more alive when we were together. And I never felt more at peace.

This wasn't a good idea. Tomorrow morning it would probably be a regret. But I couldn't stop myself. I wanted this more than anything, to have just one night with her. I wanted to forget about the next day and all the heartbreak it would bring.

I scooped her into my arms and carried her into my bedroom. Our kisses were still slow and soft. When they parted a light smacking noise filled the air. Kissing her was the biggest turn on because she was so good at it. I loved the way her small tongue felt against mine.

I slowly undressed her while my mouth was glued to hers. I wanted to see her body but I wanted to kiss her more. I got the dress unzipped and loose from her body. Then I pulled it off, taking her bra and panties too.

She wrapped her legs around my waist as she pulled off my shirt, kissing me with the same intensity as before. Then her hands moved to my jeans, unbuttoning them and removing them.

Friday

I got my boxers off, kicking them to the side as quickly as possible. All I wanted was to be inside her, to fall into a world where nothing else could follow. She was the only thing that could make me forget the ghosts that haunted me.

I positioned myself on top of her and got ready to feel that connection, that overwhelming pleasure that made me forget everything else. I didn't want to screw her. I wanted to make love to her, and have her make love to me in return.

"Stop." She placed her hand on my chest.

I was just about to enter her but stopped when she asked. "What is it, baby?"

"I just can't do this." She scooted back, pulling herself away from me.

I hid my disappointment. "Is everything okay?"

"I can't do this knowing you have a girlfriend. It's just wrong."

A girlfriend? What? "I don't have a girlfriend."

She stopped being hesitant and immediately turned angry. "Axel, don't lie to me. That's the worst thing you can possibly do."

"I'm not lying." If I had a girlfriend, it would be her.

"I know you're seeing Alexia."

"Yuck." I blurted it out automatically. She was a troll compared to Marie. "I'm not seeing her. I haven't been with her since before you and I got together. Where the hell are you getting this from?"

"Then why was she in your apartment a few weeks ago?" Despite her nakedness she looked terrifying.

In my apartment? Alexia hadn't been in my apartment since... "How did you know that?"

"I came by to talk to you and she opened the door."

She opened the door? Why didn't she tell me? I'd never been more confused in my life. "Why didn't you come inside? Why didn't you tell me you came by?"

"Because that skank told me you were her boyfriend and I needed to stop showing my face."

"What?" I snapped. "She said that?"

"Yes."

Why would Alexia say that? "But it's not true."

"Well, she thought so."

"The only reason why she was there was because she needed a place to crash. Her roommate's boyfriend was at her place and she wasn't comfortable. She just showed up on my doorstep and I couldn't turn her away. I swear, nothing happened. I don't know why she made all that shit up."

Marie's anger dimmed away. Her eyes didn't look so threatening, and her body relaxed. "Then why did she say that?"

I shrugged. "I don't have a clue. She did ask me out a few times but I turned her down. Maybe she was getting back at me by scaring you off."

"She knew we were broken up."

I couldn't lie about that. "I told her…"

Marie crossed her arms over her chest.

"I swear, I'm not seeing her and haven't been seeing her in the past. I wouldn't lie to you."

"I know…" Her arms still covered her chest, as if she felt like she was on display.

Despite the argument we just had, I still wanted her. I hadn't been with anyone since we broke up, and if she'd been with Jason, I didn't care. It didn't change the way I felt. And if she was still seeing him, I didn't care either. She was mine, as far as I was concerned.

I moved back up her body and positioned myself on top of her. My lips hovered a fraction of an inch away from hers. She was close enough to feel my breaths fall on her face. Her body tensed all over again when I drew close to her, and slowly her arms pulled away from her chest, moving to my arms that were pinned on either side of her body.

I gave her a slow kiss, closed-mouthed and soft. I let everything wash over me, feeling her tits pressed to mine. Her chest rose with the breath she took, and I could feel it expand against me.

I moved my lips to her ear and pulled her closer to me. "Can I make love to you?" She told me to stop before, and I didn't want to pressure her into something she still didn't want.

"Please."

A shiver moved down my spine at her words. The heat in her voice moved me, made me feel alive. My cock found her entrance like it knew its way there. I felt the wetness between her legs and knew she still wanted me.

My hand returned to her hair, my favorite place, and I fisted the strands like they belonged to me. I slowly slid inside her, feeling the familiar tightness. I recognized every inch of her, having been there so many times before. It felt good, better than it ever had. It'd been six weeks since I'd had sex, and my body immediately appreciated every second of the experience.

She breathed deeply, every breath coming out as a small whisper. Her hands clung to my back, pulling me further into her. She needed me as much as I needed her.

The second I was inside her, I felt better. It wasn't the physical pleasure that felt so good. It was much more than that. The pains and aches throughout my heart were patched up with her essence. The scars that marked my body faded away. She fixed all the leaks and holes, putting me back together. It was the greatest high I'd ever known. All those nights I slept alone in my truck faded away. It felt like we'd never been apart. It was just she and I— like we'd always been this way.

I kissed her jawline and her neck as I moved inside her, treasuring the taste of her on my tongue. My lips memorized every inch of her skin, knowing exactly where everything was by touch alone. I buried my face in her neck and listened to her moan for me, loving the way I felt inside her. I stretched her in a good way, giving her the kind of pleasure she deserved.

Her nails dragged down my back, cutting into the skin in a sexy way. She panted hard at the same time, breathless and excited.

Whenever she touched me, it was with need and not desire. She made me feel loved without a single word. She cared about me in a way no woman ever had. I didn't feel like a hot guy she picked up in a bar. I felt like something more—something worthwhile. The first time we hooked up seemed to be forgotten. It was like it never happened at all. It never should have happened at all.

I should have made love to her from the beginning.

Friday

CHAPTER EIGHTEEN

Dreams

Marie

For the past few weeks my body felt like it'd been in a car wreck. It was smashed and crushed, broken beyond repair. Everything hurt even when I didn't move.

But now everything was fixed.

I could breathe easy again, feel the air enter my lungs then exist slowly. All the despair that weighed on my shoulders seemed to have disappeared. Now that Axel was back in my life, lying beside me in that very moment, I didn't have a care in the world.

Axel was wrapped tightly around me, his powerful chest humming like a low-burning engine. With every breath it expanded against me, lulling me into a place of tranquility. The little things he did in bed brought back great memories. The way he sighed just when he readjusted himself still carried on. Sometimes he would snore but it only last a few minutes before he turned his head and stopped. And he never released his hold on me in the middle of night. That was something that never changed.

I had to get up and get to class. I already blew off school yesterday, and Axel couldn't blow off another day at the office even though he would try. I glanced at the clock on the nightstand and knew I needed to get going.

But it was so hard to leave him.

Axel woke up a moment later, his brain naturally programmed to stir when his alarm was supposed to go off. He stared at the side of my face then leaned in and kissed me on the cheek. "Morning, beautiful."

"Morning."

He kissed the back of my neck then my shoulder. "I haven't slept that well in a long time..."

"Me neither."

He kissed my shoulder again. "I wish we could stay in this bed all day..."

"I do too. But our responsibilities await us."

"Eh." He pressed a kiss to the skin between my shoulder blades. "You have the most beautiful skin."

"Thank you..."

"Actually, you have the most beautiful everything."

"Thank you again."

He leaned over me and pressed a kiss to my ear. "I'm going to shower. Wanna join me?"

"I should get home. All my stuff is there." I'd have to bring a bag of my things so I could stay there on the weekends. Francesca seemed to be self-efficient at this point. Whether Cameron was around or not, she would be fine.

"Alright." He got out of bed, his hard body looking powerful. Then he pulled on his boxers and t-shirt. "I'll walk you out."

I pulled on the clothes I wore the night before and tried not to cringe at the walk of shame I was about to perform. Francesca would have a million questions, and I'd have to answer them without making her throw up.

Axel walked me to the door then cupped my cheeks, staring hard into my face. His thumbs rested on the corners of my mouth. "Last night was fun."

"It was."

He pressed his forehead to mine. "Thank you...for everything."

"You don't need to thank me. I'll always be here for you."

Friday

"I know." He moved his lips to my forehead and gave me a soft kiss, a kind of kiss he'd never given me before. His lips lingered for a long time, feeling searing hot against my skin. "And I'll always be here for you."

***

Francesca was just about to leave for class when I walked in. "Tell me everything."

"Can I come in first?"

She stepped out of the way and followed me all the way into the kitchen. "Same clothes...messy hair...stupid smile. I can connect the dots."

"Then connect them so I don't have to talk about it."

"Did you...?" She didn't ask the full question because it was too awkward to say it out loud.

I nodded.

Francesca clapped. "About damn time. Shit, you guys took forever."

"Good things are worth waiting for."

"So, you guys are back together?"

"Yep."

"Great. Now everyone is happy. What are the odds of that?"

I poured a mug of coffee and added a splash of cream. "Everything feels right again. I knew something was different yesterday. Maybe forgiving your father loosened him up."

"Maybe," she said. "I'm glad you got him to go. No one could have pulled that off but you."

I made a piece of toast and ate it at the counter.

"What did you do, exactly?"

"Nothing really," I said. "I just asked him to."

"Bullshit," she said. "There must have been something else to it."

I remembered the words he said right before that. They were an accident but I still heard them. "He said he would never abandon his kids like that. Then he said even if I died he would still be there for them..."

"You? As in, the future mother of his kids?"

I nodded.

"Awe..." She clapped her hands in a way she hadn't done in a long time. "That's so great. I'm so glad he finally came out and said it. It's so obvious how he feels about you."

I was glad he finally admitted it too. "At least this story has a happy ending."

"A great ending," she said. "But I have a feeling there's more to the story." She looked at the time on the coffee pot. "I want to hear more about it when I get home, alright?"

I rolled my eyes. "Yes, Mom."

She gave me the finger before she walked out.

I finished my coffee then poured the rest out in the sink. There was a pile of dirty dishes, and since I was in a good mood I decided to do them. After I stacked the dishes in the dishwasher, I looked out the small window over the sink.

Hawke was walking across the lawn.

What the hell?

I quickly dried my hands and threw down the towel. "What does he want?" I walked to the door and opened it before he even knocked. "You just missed her." He had to be there for her. What other reason would he have?

"Again, I'm not here for her."

I kept the disappointment from creeping into my features. "Then what do you want?"

He walked in without being invited. The first thing he did was examine the Spackle he placed over the hole in the wall. He felt it with his fingers before he turned back to me.

"Hawke, just spit it out. I don't want you to stink up the house."

"Excuse me?"

"Last time you were here, Francesca could smell you."

His cold stare changed slightly. Panic entered his eyes. "She knew I was here?"

"I told her a handyman fixed the wall and he must wear your cologne. But she swore it wasn't cologne—it was you." If I hadn't witnessed their relationship first hand, I would have thought she was crazy. But they had some sort of connection where they could sense each other, even if they weren't in the same room at the same time.

"Fuck." He sighed in frustration then opened the door. "Let's talk outside."

I followed him onto the lawn. "What's up? Francesca might come back so hurry."

"She won't. I waited a few minutes to make sure."

I looked around for his truck but didn't see it anywhere. "Where's your truck?"

"I have a car now. And it's down the street."

Now I understood why Francesca hadn't spotted him. If he were in his truck she would have immediately noticed him.

"I just wanted to see how she's doing. I'd ask Axel but she's still a touchy subject for him."

"She's been a lot better. It seems like she really likes Cameron."

His eyes quickly looked away, trying to hide the pain that burned right on the surface. He tried to brush it off, to bottle it deep inside, but I could tell that revelation bothered him. "I meant yesterday. Her father's anniversary."

He remembered? "She was pretty sad...like usual."

"Did you go to the cemetery with her?"

"No, but she, Axel, and I were there at the same time."

"Axel went?" He placed his hands in his pockets.

"Yeah..." *Thanks to me.*

Hawke understood the significance. "I'm glad you guys got back together."

"That makes two of us." I kept the smile off my face because he seemed miserable. It just wasn't right to be happy when he was barely keeping himself together.

"So, she's okay?"

"Yeah." Why did he care so much about her father's anniversary and not her mother's? "She visited her mother two weeks ago..." Maybe he forgot. Or maybe he just didn't know.

"I know. I was there. She seemed okay."

"You were there?" I blurted.

"She didn't see me."

How could she not see him at an empty cemetery? "If you're still keeping tabs on her, why don't you just get back together with her?"

Hawke acted as though he hadn't heard a word I said. "I was stuck at the office yesterday and I couldn't come down. I'm glad she's doing okay. If she went to school today, then she must be fine."

"She is."

"Well...that's all I wanted to know. Thanks for answering my questions."

Times like this made me hate him. He had no right to check on her wellbeing like it was any of his business, not when he left her so coldly. It was a complete paradox. He loved her but refused to be with her. "Hawke, don't come back here anymore. I mean it."

He turned back to me when he heard the threat.

"You can't have it both ways. You can't skip town and leave her behind but expect to be involved in her life. You can't snoop around and watch her from a safe distance. If you care that much about her, just be with her. Otherwise, you're just being nosy."

Hawke wasn't as emotional as Axel. He kept the same demeanor no matter how angry he was. "I'm not being nosy. I don't expect you to understand what exists between Francesca and me. Just because we aren't together anymore doesn't mean I don't care about her. I will always care about her. She doesn't see me and she has no idea that I'm here. So, there's no problem."

"She smelled you, Hawke. Do you understand how weird that is? She took one step in the house and immediately knew. I had to spend ten minutes convincing her she was crazy."

Hawke took a step back. "Well, we won't have that problem again. Good bye, Marie."

"Bye, Hawke," I said coldly.

He turned away and walked off, heading down the street to wherever his car was parked.

In my heart, I knew Hawke was a good person. He came all the way down here to help out Axel, and when he checked on Francesca his heart was in the right place.

But I would always hate him for what he did to Francesca.

***

I sat at the kitchen table and kept the blinds open, loving the beautiful sunset going on right outside my window. My laptop was open with an article I was writing but my heart wasn't in it. I kept thinking about Axel. My phone sat next to my hand, and I anxiously waited for it to ring.

I wanted to see him.

Francesca's car drove on the street then pulled into the driveway. She had class and work, so she was getting home later than usual. With her backpack over her shoulder she walked across the lawn and approached the porch.

I watched her, remembering the way Hawke stood outside just a few hours before. He was constantly with her, lurking in the shadows unseen, and she had no idea she was being watched.

She suddenly halted before the stoop, staring at something I couldn't see. She was still as a statue, her face becoming pale. Then she looked around, searching for something I couldn't see. She stood there for several minutes, searching and listening for something.

Did she know?

Her face was expressionless as she waited, using all of her senses to find something. After another minute she walked into the house, her face still deathly pale.

Friday

"Hey...you alright?" I rose from my chair, prepared for anything.

"Yeah...I'm fine." She dropped her backpack on the table, her eyes glued to the window.

"You seem...a little off. Did you see something?" There was no way she smelled Hawke's scent outside. Hours had passed and the smell wafted away in the spring air. There was just no way.

"I thought..." She shook her head. "Never mind."

"No, tell me." When she told me they were soul mates I thought she was just being a hopeless romantic. I never believed her, but now I wasn't so sure.

"It's hard to explain...have you ever walked into a room or a place and knew something was different? Everything is exactly the same but not really? The porch just seemed...different. Like something or someone out of place had been there."

I crossed my arms over my chest. "Not really."

"It was almost like...never mind." She walked around me and headed to the fridge.

"No, I want to know."

"You'll think I'm weird."

"I already do. But tell me anyway."

She grabbed a bottle of water and shut the door. "I just feel him. Like he was there or something."

"Who's him?" This couldn't be happening.

"Hawke..."

My mind was officially blown. How did she know that? How could she tell? He was there for ten minutes before he left. There wasn't enough time to taint the air, the plants, or anything else in the area.

But somehow she knew.

Maybe she was right all along. Maybe whatever they had was beyond human understanding. Maybe what they had really was special. Maybe their souls really originated from the same place and they found each other on this earth. Once they touched they were constantly connected—near and far.

***

Axel didn't call me yesterday, which I thought was strange. We just got back together so didn't he want to be with me all the time? I missed him like crazy even though I just had him. He didn't feel the same way?

Maybe I was reading too much into it. He probably had to work late and had a lot to catch up on. On top of that, he had his own interviews to prepare for. My interview with Prada was tomorrow afternoon and I tried not to freak out about it. If I got that job it would change my life forever. And if I didn't get it, it would change my life forever.

"I'm surprised Axel isn't here." Francesca just finished showering and drying her hair. Her face was free of makeup and she wore shorts and a t-shirt.

"Me too."

"Is he coming over tonight? Are you going over there?"

"I haven't heard from him."

Francesca raised both eyebrows before she walked into the kitchen and made a peanut butter and jelly sandwich. "That's strange. I figured you guys would be all over each other, all the time."

"That makes two of us. I'm sure he'll call."

Like he'd been listening, my phone lit up with a text message.

"There we go," Francesca said. "The greatest love affair of all time begins…"

I read the message. *Hey. Can I come over?*

Did he really need to ask*? Of course.*

We should prepare for the interview tomorrow. I really want you to get it.

"Awe..."

"What?" Francesca asked.

"He wants to coach my interview skills so I get the job."

"This sweet side of him is one I'm not used to." She took a big bite of her sandwich, getting peanut butter everywhere.

I texted him back. *Come over whenever.*

Want me to pick up dinner on the way?

Pizza wouldn't be the worst thing ever.

You got it.

"He's coming over now and bringing a pizza."

"Ugh and yay," she said. "I don't want to watch you two make out all the time. But I wouldn't mind a pizza."

I liked watching her eat. For months she didn't take a bite of anything. Now she was an eating machine just like before. "Get used to it. I suspect there will be a lot of kissing."

"Yuck."

***

Axel used his key to get inside. "It's me."

"The pizza delivery boy," Francesca said with fake enthusiasm.

"If that's the case, I better get a tip." He walked inside and set the box on the table.

"How about this for a tip?" Francesca gave him the bird.

I rose from my chair when he walked inside, excited for a hug and the kind of kiss that would make me weak in the knees.

Axel walked right past me and headed to the fridge. "I need a beer." He grabbed a bottle then twisted off the cap.

That was weird.

"I've never had an interview for an editorial position before but I can only assume they'll ask the same generic questions." He grabbed a paper plate from the top of the fridge then fell into the chair, immediately taking a few slices out of the box.

I stood there awkwardly, unsure what to do.

Francesca glanced back and forth between us, just as confused as I was.

Axel pulled his laptop out of his bag and set it up on the table. "I have a lot of good stuff we can use for this. You'll be so prepared they'll think you're interviewing them." He looked up at me and gave me a smile before he turned back to the computer.

Francesca was the one who spoke up. "Is that how you greet your girlfriend? Or is it just because I'm here?"

Axel looked at her in confusion. "What?"

"You just walked in here and didn't kiss me or anything," I said. "Are you okay?"

Axel glanced back and forth between us, like he had no idea what was going on. "Why would I do that...?"

I crossed my arms over my chest, starting to worry if I dreamt that whole night.

Francesca stopped eating and began to look uncomfortable. "I just remembered I have to shower...because I smell." She left the kitchen as quickly as she could without running.

Axel watched her go before he turned back to me. "Marie..."

"What the hell is going on?" First, he said I was the future mother of his children and then he slept with me. And now he was going to act like nothing happened?

"I thought we both agreed that was a one-time thing." He slowly rose to his feet.

"When did we agree to that?" I couldn't keep my voice down because I was pissed. *Actually, I was beyond pissed.*

"Nothing has changed. I still can't be what you need me to be—"

Friday

"You said I was the future mother of your children." *Who the hell just says that?*

"Look, that just slipped out. I was depressed and I was just talking—"

"And you were being yourself—honest and true. How can you say something like that but not tell me you love me?" It made no sense whatsoever. I was sick of his bullshit. He was taking me for another ride.

"Listen to me—"

"And then you slept with me. You initiated all of that and you acted like it actually meant something." I couldn't stop myself from screaming. I wasn't just hurt at this point. I was livid.

"It did mean something," he argued. "Of course it did."

"But then we go back to just being friends? Or whatever the hell we are?"

"I'm sorry," he said. "I thought you knew that was just a one-time thing. I had a difficult time that day and I wanted to feel better—"

"By using me?"

His eyes darkened. "No. I didn't use you, Marie."

"You fucked me but don't want to be with me. Yes, you used me. I'm not some dog that will just wait around until you want to play.

I'm a human being with feelings, Axel. I told you I loved you, that I still loved you, and then you made me believe you felt the same way. Then the next day it's like nothing happened."

"Marie—"

"Fuck you, Axel."

He took a deep breath like I just slapped him.

"I'm done with you. I'm done with this." I pointed between us. "I'm officially done."

"Marie, I didn't fuck you. I made love to you—like I always do. It's not the same thing and you know it."

"But you still tossed me aside like I didn't matter. It's the same thing in my eyes." I snatched his computer and shoved it into his bag before I pushed it into his chest. "Get the hell out, Axel."

"It wasn't like that. I thought you were in the same boat."

I wanted to slap him. "Axel, what boat is that? The slut boat? You think I don't use a condom with just any guy I sleep with? I thought what we had was special, that there was something more there besides using each other to feel better. You disgust me, Axel."

"Marie, it wasn't like that. I haven't been with anyone besides you. I just can't—"

Friday

I held up my hand to silence him. "I don't want to hear your excuses, Axel. That's all they are—excuses."

He gripped the backpack in front of his chest.

"Get out. Now."

He remained rooted to the spot like he might say something else. His eyes held my gaze before they looked at the ground. A frustrated sigh escaped his lips, one directed at me.

"Good bye, Axel." This was the last time I would look at him this way. This was the last time I would allow my heart to love him. It didn't matter how much I cared about him. I refused to be treated like this. I wasn't some girl he could just pick up and drop whenever he felt like it. I was worth a lot more than that—even if he didn't agree.

CHAPTER NINETEEN

Screw Up

Axel

I hate myself.

No. I really hate myself.

How did I misread her? Why did I sleep with her when I knew she still loved me? Why did I give into my needs instead of putting hers first? Why did I have to screw up over and over?

I thought it was clear last night was a one-time thing. And when I said that thing about the kids...I never meant for her to hear that. I wish I could take it back instead of letting her get the wrong idea.

Now I felt worse than I did the other day.

Marie was one of the most important people to me. I adored her—absolutely and pathetically. But I couldn't give her what she wanted. I should have kept that in mind before I broke her heart all over again.

Friday

Now she hated me.

And I didn't blame her.

The last time we spoke she was so angry she couldn't see straight. She screamed at me then kicked me out of the house. Her interview was today and I hoped I didn't botch it for her. The last thing she needed was to stress over an asshole like me.

I headed to the house to see if she'd come home yet. Now that she had enough time to calm down we could have a better conversation than the last one we had. I could convince her I wasn't trying to use her. Being with her meant something to me. It always meant something to me. She wasn't just a warm body in a bed. Letting her think that hurt me more than words could ever explain. Those nights we spent together were beautiful and holy. I couldn't let her taint them with misinterpretation.

I rang the doorbell instead of just walking inside like I usually did. Marie's car wasn't in the driveway but she would probably be home any minute.

Francesca opened the door, looking pissed. "You really shouldn't show your face around here for a while."

"I want to talk to her when she gets home."

"Well, neither one of us want to talk to you."

I'd push her out of the way if I had to. "Frankie, let me explain. She got it all wrong."

"How did she get it wrong?" She crossed her arms over her chest, looking remarkably similar to her childhood when she would steal something from my room and refuse to give it back. "If you don't want to get back together with her, then she got everything perfectly right. Unless you're here to say otherwise?"

"I thought she understood what that night meant."

"And why would you make such an assumption?" Francesca was fiercely protective of Marie. If I really did something to hurt her, she'd kill me.

"Because we went to see my father's grave...I was in a dark place. Come on, what do people do when they're depressed? They usually get laid and eat a bag of Cheetos."

"And you took advantage of Marie because you knew she would give that to you—because she loves you. And that's what makes you such a pathetic excuse for a human being."

Spit flew out of her mouth because she was talking so fast.

"It wasn't like that—"

"That's exactly what you said."

"No, it's not. You're twisting my words around."

"No, I'm not. And that's the sad part. You knew exactly what you were doing and you did it anyway."

We kept arguing on the front door step, and by now the neighbors must have noticed. "Look, I haven't slept with anyone but Marie since the first time I had her. Whether we've been together or apart, I've been faithful to her. It's not like I'm going around sleeping with anything that moves. I thought that night was just a break from the distance we constantly kept from each other, but it's not like she was just some piece of ass. If that's all I wanted I could have gotten that from anyone. Marie is different. With Marie—"

"You. Love. Her." She stomped her foot with every syllable. "When the hell will you get that through your tiny brain? It's written all over your face. It's obvious in everything you do. Stop dragging my girl through the mud and just admit how you feel about her. Just be with her, Axel. Shit, it's not that hard."

"I don't love her." I was getting tired of repeating that.

She gripped her skull and tried not to scream. "Axel...I swear to god I'm going to kill you."

"If I did, I would admit it. Why would I keep lying?"

"Maybe you don't understand what love is even though it's looking you right in the face this very moment."

"I can't give Marie what she deserves. I'm not going to waste her time trying."

"So, you're going to yank her around on a leash until you finally decide to let her go? Axel, what you're doing to her now is way worse than anything you could possibly do to her as her boyfriend."

I put my hands in my pocket and watched the road, hoping she would come home soon.

"Axel, she's pissed. Actually, she's whatever comes after pissed. I've never seen her this mad. You're on the verge of losing her for good. You've broken her heart too many times. Honestly, I think you're too late even if you changed your mind right this second. She's going to see other guys—really see them—and she's going to get over you. By the time you wake up from this stupid dream of yours it's going to be too late. And then you'll really know what it's like to lose someone."

I kept my eyes on the street, not wanting to listen to her anymore. Her car appeared down the road, and as the seconds passed it came closer and closer. Instead of pulling into the driveway she stopped the car right at the curb. She took one look at us, wearing aviator sunglasses with an obvious frown on her lips, and then hit the gas and took off again.

"Go home, Axel." Francesca walked inside and shut the door in my face.

I stood on the porch and watched her car disappear down the road. When I could no longer see it, I knew she wasn't coming back anytime soon. Not when I was here.

I took a seat on the stoop and rested my arms on my knees. If I had to wait all day I would. She'd come back eventually.

And I would be here waiting.

***

Later that night she pulled into the driveway. But she wasn't alone.

A man was in the passenger seat, the same guy I saw her with at the restaurant.

They got out of the car and walked to the front door. Marie took off her sunglasses, revealing terrifying eyes. She had murder written all over her face. She wanted to bury me six feet under. "It's so annoying when people leave their dogs on your property..."

I ignored the jab, and I ignored the guy she was with. "Marie, let me talk."

"You said everything you needed to say yesterday."

"You were upset and you weren't listening to me."

"Oh, I listened to you." Her voice raised a few octaves. "And I don't feel like listening to you again. Jason and I are on a date. Well, we're going into my bedroom to have sex. But same difference, right?" She walked around me and headed to the front door.

"Marie, please give me five minutes."

"Why?" She turned around and glared at me.

Jason stood there but stayed out of the way. It didn't seem like he wanted anything to do with this conversation, and he didn't seem jealous by me either. It made me wonder what kind of relationship they really had.

"Why should I listen to you?" she snapped. "This can wait for another day. Right now, I'm busy."

Friday

"I don't want you to screw some guy just because you're mad at me."

"Well, I don't want you to screw me just because you're depressed. We don't always get what we want." She unlocked the door and walked inside. She was so angry she wouldn't listen to reason. Now I wish I hadn't come over. If she hadn't seen me on the porch, she wouldn't have picked up Jason.

I blocked his path so he couldn't get inside. "Please go. I'll give you a ride."

"What?" He looked at me like I was a crazy person.

"You can't sleep with her. Not when she's like this. Come on, it wouldn't be right. Don't do that to her."

"Jason, don't listen to him," Marie said. "Come inside."

"Please." I was practically begging at this point. "She's not in her right mind. She's only doing this to get back at me."

"Dude." He pushed me back. "If you really cared that much about who Marie sleeps with, you'd be with her. You aren't getting any pity from me." He walked around me and joined Marie inside the house.

Marie gave me one final look before she shut the door in my face. "Good night, Axel."

CHAPTER TWENTY

It's A New Day
Marie

I threw my purse on the table so hard it slid across the surface and fell on the other side.

Francesca shut the blinds to the window so Axel couldn't see into the house. A grimace similar to my own was on her face. "I just want to slap him..."

Jason stood there with his hands in his pockets, remaining silent.

"He's such an ass," I snapped. "What did I ever see in him?"

"I tried telling you that in the beginning," Francesca said. "But did you listen to me? No."

Now I wish I had.

"Come on, Jason. Let's go have sex." I grabbed his hand and yanked him down the hallway.

Friday

"Uh...alright." He followed me into my bedroom and shut the door behind him.

I slipped off my heels then removed my jacket. "Let's get to it."

Jason sat at the foot of the bed, still clothed. He watched me with expressionless eyes.

"What are you doing?" I grabbed the hem of his shirt and tried to pull it off.

"Marie, sit down." He grabbed my wrists gently and pulled them away. "Come on, let's talk."

"Talk dirty?" I sat beside him and felt the bed bounce underneath me.

"We aren't having sex."

"Why the hell not?" I pulled Jason in the house just for that reason. I wanted to get back at Axel, to hurt him the way he hurt me. I was tired of letting him walk all over me, breaking me apart over and over.

"Marie, do you honestly want to have sex with me?" He watched my expression, his eyes already containing my answer. "I didn't think so. As much as I enjoy sex, I really don't want to be with a woman who's thinking about another man."

Embarrassed, I looked away.

"And it sounds like something happened between you guys..."

I hadn't told Jason we slept together. "I went to his place because he was going through a hard time. One thing led to another and we spent the night together. I thought we got back together, but to him, it was just a booty call." Jason and I weren't exclusive but he had a right to know where I slept at night—and whom I slept with.

He didn't seem hurt or disappointed, but the news was significant to him. "Marie, I like you. I think you're pretty and smart. We have a great time together. But I really don't want to get caught up in anything..."

I didn't blame him for feeling that way. "I understand, Jason."

"It doesn't seem like this relationship with Axel is over. I'll never have a chance under these conditions. I'm not a romantic guy, but I don't want to keep competing against a guy I'll never beat."

"It is over," I said. "But you have every right to feel that way." Jason and I were never serious but the relationship didn't start off right. We never had a chance because I never gave it a chance. I kept thinking about Axel, hoping our love would rekindle instead of focusing on the great guy in front of me.

"I don't understand what's going on between you. But it seems like you need to forget about him."

"I know..."

"Give it some time to die down. Move on and find yourself. When you come to a good place give me a call. But for now, I think I have to take a step back."

"I don't blame you." He'd already dumped me three times now.

"What is it with this guy, Marie?"

I sighed in embarrassment because I didn't have an answer. "I have no idea."

"Do you guys have a lot in common?"

"Not really."

"Are you just really attracted to him? Is it all physical?"

"I am really attracted to him. But no, it's not physical at all."

"Then what is it?"

"If I knew I would tell you. If I could describe it, I would. But I can't."

"Surely, you must know why you love him."

I thought I did. But was there any concrete reason to love someone? Was it a combination of things? Or was it just a choice? I'd never been in love prior to this so I didn't really know. "I do...but I also don't."

"Well, it doesn't seem like he appreciates it."

"No, he doesn't." There was no denying that fact. Axel captured my heart the moment our lips touched for the first time. His compassion and sensitivity brought me to my knees. When it was just he and I everything seemed perfect. I could picture us growing old together, surrounded by our children and grandchildren. When I pictured my husband's face, it was Axel.

But he claimed he didn't feel the same way.

"Marie, you're too beautiful and smart to put up with a guy like him. I suggest you move on and forget about him."

I stared at my hands in my lap. "I couldn't agree more."

"Stop seeing him so you can get over him. And when that day finally happens, start dating again."

"If I get that job I'll be moving to New York in a month."

"There you go. There's plenty of fish in the sea—especially the New York Sea."

I chuckled. "You're probably right."

"So...can we be friends?" He extended his hand to shake mine.

"I'd love to be your friend." I took it before I dropped his embrace.

"Great. I'm glad we could work this out."

"Me too."

He looked around my room, eyeing my bookshelves and dressers. He spotted my desk in the corner. It was made of white wood, vintage and handcrafted. "So...what do you want to do?"

I shrugged. "We can get dinner. My treat."

"I am hungry..."

I didn't have an appetite since Axel stabbed me in the heart, but it was slowly coming back. "How about pizza and Putt-Putt golf?"

He smiled. "That sounds awesome."

***

Axel didn't come around for the next week, which was nice since I didn't want to see him anyway. I needed a break from him and all the drama that accompanied him. I wasn't looking for a husband when we got together, but I also wasn't looking for a meaningless fling either. Now I realized we both wanted different things and I needed to move on with my life. If Francesca could move on from Hawke, then I could do this.

"You doing okay?" Francesca served the plate of fajitas in front of me.

"I'm better." *A little bit, at least.*

"Has he called?"

"No. Thankfully."

She sat across from me and took a bite of her burrito. "At least he understands you need space."

"Actually, he just understands I'm not going to let him play me anymore."

Francesca ate and kept her eyes on me. She didn't defend her brother even though he was her family. That told me he really deserved it. "At least you have Jason. He's nice."

"We actually went our separate ways."

"Why?"

"He wasn't comfortable with the whole Axel thing, and I honestly can't blame him. He didn't want to get in the middle of something so complicated."

"Are you okay?"

"Yeah, I'm fine. He made the right decision. He shouldn't have to go through that."

"Well...at least we're graduating soon."

"Yeah. Then I'll be able to get out of here and never see Axel again."

Francesca gave me a sad look before she kept eating. "I can't believe the semester is almost over...and I'm actually going to pass my classes."

My phone rang on the table and I saw a number I didn't recognize. The area code was from New York.

Francesca leaned forward and looked at it. "Do you think it's from a place you applied to?"

"I hope so." My heartbeat kicked into overdrive as I stared at the screen. It could be a callback from a magazine, or it could just be another rejection.

"What if it's Prada?'"

"Now you're really making me nervous."

"Girl, you've got this." She dropped her burrito on the plate. "Own it."

I took a deep breath before I answered. "Hello. This is Marie."

"Marie, this is Hilda from Prada. We met for an interview last week."

I covered the receiver and whispered to Francesca. "It's Prada."

She drummed her hands on the table in excitement. "Oh my god. Oh my god."

I returned the phone back to my ear. "It's nice to hear from you, Hilda. Thanks so much for meeting with me last week." My manners kicked in on autopilot.

"The pleasure was all mine, Ms. Prescott. I'm calling because we were hoping you could come down for another interview."

I covered my mouth so I wouldn't scream.

Francesca stood up, desperately wanting to know what was being said.

I put my hand down. "I'd love to."

"Great. I know this is short notice, but are you available tomorrow?"

I had econ class but I didn't give a damn about that. "I'm open."

"Great. We'll see you at two."

"Thanks so much, Hilda. See you then."

"Goodbye." She hung up.

"Oh my god!" I jumped up and down and knocked over the chair. I needed some good news after all the shit Axel put me through.

"What'd she say? Talk to me!"

"I got a second interview." I let out a scream.

"Oh my god. Are you serious?"

"Yes!"

Friday

"I knew this would happen. You're so going to get that job."

"God, I hope so."

"When is this happening?"

"Tomorrow."

"Damn, that's short notice. Don't you have class?"

"Who cares? It's not like I have an exam."

"True."

I started to pace back and forth. "Oh my god. I'm not going to be able to sleep tonight."

"Me neither."

"I'm going to have to take some Nyquil or something."

"Or Ativan if we had it."

I headed to my bedroom. "I need to pick out my outfit and change it a million times."

"Let me help you." We both abandoned our dinner and headed to my room, doing what we do best. Together, we picked out the best outfit with just the right shoes. Now that I was excited about something I couldn't stop thinking about Axel for just a few moments. It didn't last long, but that short amount of time still gave me some peace.

***

Even though I already had one interview, I was nervous as hell. My leg wouldn't stop shaking and my heart wouldn't slow down. There were very few things I wanted this much, and right now this job was at the top of the list.

Hilda asked me a few more questions about my interests in writing and where I pictured myself in the next five years. She took interest in my clothes, noticing the Prada shoes I wore. Then the interview came to an end.

"Thank you for coming down here today. I'm excited to give this to you." She grabbed an envelope from her drawer and pushed it across the table toward me. "I think you'll find that we offer a competitive salary with benefits. Think things over and get back to me."

I stared at the envelope without taking it, unable to believe what she just said. "Whoa...what?"

She gave me a friendly smile then glanced at the envelope.

"Are you offering me the job?" I'd been on very few job interviews, especially professional ones like this. Was this how they hired people? With a letter?

"Yes. That's why we called you down here today."

I took the envelope with shaky hands then opened it. The letter showed my salary for the year, along with my benefit plans, my number of sick days, and my vacation hours.

Oh my god.

"Get back to us within a week," Hilda said. "I hope you'll be joining us here at Prada."

Somehow, I kept my cool and didn't scream. "I'll take it."

"Are you sure you don't want some time to think it over?"

"Absolutely not." There was no better job out there. This was exactly what I wanted. I didn't need time to think it over. "I can start the day after I graduate."

She smiled. "I'm glad to hear your excitement."

"Thank you so much for giving me the opportunity. I won't let you down."

"Stacy had nothing but good things to say about you. Personally, I care more about a person's drive, personality, and determination than where they went to school and what their G.P.A. is. It's clear you share the same passion as the rest of us. I think you'll be a good fit here."

I wanted to scream all over again. "Thank you so much." I stood up and shook her hand.

"See you next month." She gave me a friendly smile before she sat back down.

I waved then walked out, holding my head high and keeping my shoulders back. After I left the building and reached my car in the parking garage I finally let out the scream I'd been holding back. I called Francesca. "Oh my god. I got the job. I actually got the job. I'm officially working at Prada." I said the words as quickly as possible. It was incoherent but Francesca would decipher it.

"Holy shit! I'm so happy for you."

"I know...I'm happy for me too."

"Get your ass back here so we can go out."

"I'm on my way."

***

"I can't believe this," Francesca said. "You got a job and you aren't even out of college yet."

"I can't believe it either." I just finished my third margarita and I didn't need another one.

"That means you're going to have to find a place fast. Like, pronto."

"I know. But I should be able to get a good place in the city. I can afford it." My paycheck would allow me to have the lifestyle I wanted. I didn't have to have a roommate anymore and I could still afford to go out a few times a week. "But it'll be weird not living with you anymore..."

"I know." She pouted her lips in sadness. "It'll be strange."

"No more muffins in the middle of the night."

"Well, I'm sure I'll still make you a ton. They just won't be fresh at 3 A. M."

"What are you going to do?" I'd keep paying rent until she found someone else to shack up with her.

"I don't think I'm going to stay here."

"Really?" I asked in surprise.

"I've always wanted to move to New York anyway. That's where my shop is going to be. I may as well start scouting. There's nothing left for me here anyway."

"What about Cameron?" I thought they were hitting it off.

"I like him and everything but I'm not willing to stick around for him. I'm not sure what he plans to do after graduation. He doesn't seem motivated to do a lot."

"Does that mean you would break up with him?"

"New York is too far to commute. So yeah."

"Oh..." I was hoping something more would come of this relationship. She didn't even sleep with him. Cameron was totally a rebound but I thought she would get some use out of him.

"I think we can still be friends. He was never very serious with me anyway. If anything, I think he was helping me through a hard time."

"What did he get out of it?"

A guilty look came over her face.

Now my job was completely forgotten. "Did you...?"

She nodded.

"You slept with him?"

She nodded again. "Guilty."

"Why didn't you tell me?"

"I don't know. All that Axel shit was going on and I didn't think it was the best time to talk about my sex life."

"It's always a good time to talk about that."

"Well, we did it."

"How many times?"

"We've been doing it a lot, actually."

"That's great." It was beyond great. The fact she was sleeping with someone was an indication that everything was okay. She could still sense Hawke when he was around, but that phenomenon seemed innate. Nothing would get rid of it. "How was it?"

"The first time was terrible. All I thought about was Hawke. I kept comparing them, and then a sense of longing would overcome me. It was just sex, the kind where you try to get each other off just so you can climax. With Hawke…it was totally different. But after the first time we did it, I stopped thinking about it. Now I don't think about it at all anymore."

"That's great news."

"I like Cameron. He's a great guy and he has a lot to offer. But, I think we both understood what our relationship was. It was never going to last forever, and both of us saw the ending shortly in the distance. But that's okay. We enjoyed it while it lasted."

Why couldn't I have a healthy outlook like that? Why couldn't I take my relationship with Axel at face value? I had to be stupid and fall in love with him—like an idiot. "At least you had fun while it lasted."

"Yeah, that relationship helped me a lot. I'll always feel grateful toward him. He put up with me a lot."

"That was sweet."

"He had his own issues, and I think I helped with that. It was mutual."

"So...that means we're both moving to New York." I was so ready to get the hell out of there. I didn't want to be in the same town as Axel as much as possible. I wanted to move to the big city and see all the other fish in the sea. I wanted to find a great guy who would care for me the way I cared for him. I wanted to find a husband—someone to fall in love with. "We can be roommates again."

"Of course not," Francesca said. "You should get your own place. You deserve it."

"Where will you go?"

She shrugged. "I'll figure it out. I'm a good problem solver."

In the back of my mind, I kept thinking about Hawke. He would be living in the same city as both of us. If he kept popping up around here, he was bound to pop up around there. "And what about him...?"

She immediately had an answer, like she rehearsed it. "New York is a much bigger place than Myrtle Beach. I doubt we'll run into each other. Eight million people live there."

I wasn't so sure about that. "As long as you're okay with it."

"I wouldn't go so far as to say I'm over him." She was quiet for nearly a minute before she continued. "But I'm...okay." She nodded like she was agreeing with herself. "I'm really okay. I can picture myself with other men, and I can see myself having something with someone someday. It still hurts the way he left me, but if he's happy I'm happy for him. A part of me will always love him, but I've also let him go. I'm ready to move on to the next chapter in my life."

I'd been waiting to hear those words for a long time. "Good for you."

She grabbed her glass and held it up high. "A toast."

I grabbed my glass even though it was empty.

"To two of the most badass chicks ever."

"I'll drink to that." I clanked my glass against hers.

"And to all the hearts we're about to break in the big city." She downed her margarita and drank it all.

"Cheers."

***

It was hard to concentrate on school when I had a job waiting for me. It didn't seem like it mattered if I got A's or C's. Hilda said G. P. A. didn't matter to her. It didn't matter to me either.

Somehow, I pushed on and tried to focus. I had the most serious case of senioritis and I couldn't shake it off. In just two weeks, I would be graduating with honors and skipping town.

My life was finally taking a good turn.

I had to get all my things together as quickly as possible, and I needed to find somewhere to live. I wasn't staying in Myrtle Beach a second longer than I had to. I wanted to find a one-bedroom apartment in the city, something bigger than a broom closet. And I needed to start packing my things and sorting my stuff out from Francesca's. We'd been living together for so long I didn't know what belonged to whom at this point.

"Packing already?" Francesca watched me place the boxes behind the couch.

"I'm doing it in stages. It's better than to do it all at once, right?"

"I think you're just excited." She gave me a smile, the kind that showed her happiness for me.

"Well…I am excited."

Francesca pointed to her laptop at the table. "I found a few apartments you might like. They're close to your work so you won't have to take a cab. You can probably walk."

"Thanks, Frankie."

"No problem."

Friday

I stacked the next box on top. It was full of old clothes I didn't wear anymore. The box below it was full of shoes. The couches belonged to Francesca so I'd have to get my own stuff when I found a place. "Frankie, I really think you should live with me for a while."

"Girl, I'll be fine."

"Come on, it makes sense. It's only temporary. Stay with me for a few months while you take care of your bakery. I don't know a whole lot about business, but I know opening up a shop isn't a walk in the park."

"I don't want to burden you. You've had to put up with me for four years."

"It's been longer than that."

"You know what I mean." She put one hand on her hip. "You deserve your own space."

"I wouldn't be asking you unless I wanted you to come with me. That way you don't have to rush out and settle for something you don't love. You can take your time and not have to worry about making rent and stuff like that."

"You're sure?"

"Yes." I looked her in the eye as I said it. "Not a doubt."

"In that case, I'll live with you—again."

"Yay." I pulled her in for a hug. "Besides, this way I won't be so lonely. I'll have someone to share the adventure with."

"You'll always have me to share everything with." She pulled away and gave my wrists a squeeze. "Now, let's pick out an apartment."

***

I knew this day was coming. There was no way to avoid it, and there was never a way to avoid it. It was just the way of life. Axel was Francesca's brother, and he would always be around.

I just had to make my peace with it.

He walked inside and immediately spotted the boxes stacked behind the couch in the living room. There were a few boxes on the counter filled with kitchenware we wouldn't need for a few weeks. His eyes changed as he looked around, noticing all the differences. "Are you having a yard sale?"

"No." I grabbed a permanent marker than wrote on the side of the box. I just placed all my dishes and Tupperware inside. I hardly used the dishes anyway. Paper plates were my poison.

Axel looked around again before he turned back to me. "Then what are you doing?"

"Moving." I pushed the cap on the pen until it clicked. Then I walked passed him as if he didn't exist. "So please get out of the way. I have stuff to do."

"Whoa, hold on." He stepped in my path and prevented me from going anywhere. "You're moving? Where to?"

"New York."

"Did you get the job?"

For a second I forgot how I got that job to begin with. Axel arranged it for me. Without him, I'd still be job hunting at that very moment. Despite his generosity I was still pissed at him. He really wounded me. "Yes."

"That's great..." Instead of being happy he seemed miserable. "I knew you would get it." He swallowed the lump in his throat before he glanced at the boxes again.

"Thanks for helping me out with that..." I had to spit that out and get it over with. Showing him gratitude was harder than I imagined.

"No problem."

"Well...I should get back to work." I stepped around him.

"Wait." He got in my way again. "When is this happening?"

"A week and a half. I'm taking off right after graduation."

"That's a little sudden."

"Well, I start work the Monday after I graduate. So I need to get a move on."

"It's still rushed."

"I don't mind. I want to get out of here anyway." *Because of him.*

He rubbed the back of his neck, continuing to stare me down. "This is a lot to take in."

I was relieved I was moving away. Now I wouldn't have to see Axel anymore. If my luck worked out right, I wouldn't have to see him ever again. "Well, take your time—somewhere else." I grabbed the next cardboard piece off the table and constructed a box.

"Is Jason going with you…?"

I wanted to lie. "No."

"How does he feel about this?"

I didn't want to tell him we broke up. I wanted him to believe I was sleeping with every guy in town and I didn't give a damn about him anymore. "We stopped seeing each other."

"Oh…"

"But that works out for both of us. I'm sure I'll meet someone in the city."

Axel put his hands in his pockets.

Friday

"Axel, are you here for a reason? Because I'm very busy."

"I wanted to check on Francesca..."

"Well, she's not here. And she's fine. You don't need to check on her anymore. By the way, she's coming with me."

"What?" he blurted.

"She's moving with me to New York. She's going to stay with me for a while until she gets her plans straightened out."

He rubbed the back of his neck again.

Now that the box was made I picked it up. "Please let yourself out. I've got packing to do." I walked into my bedroom then emptied out the clothes in my drawers. I expected him to follow me, to say something else about the sudden change of plans. Deep inside me, somewhere hidden in several layers, was the hope that he might ask me to stay or ask to come with me. When I heard the front door open and close I knew that wasn't happening.

He let me go.

CHAPTER TWENTY-ONE

Detour

Axel

Marie was leaving.

I arranged that job interview because I knew how much she wanted it. Writing for Prada and going to work every day in that beautiful building would make her happy. Having a job she loved would bring excitement to her life. Instead of working as an intern for pennies, she would already start at the top. That was exactly what I wanted for her.

But now I had to say goodbye.

I knew I would make my way to New York eventually, but I wasn't sure when the move would take place. And by the time it did, Francesca wouldn't be living with her anymore. I wouldn't have a single excuse to see her. We would never bump into each other at a coffee house or the subway. It would be nearly impossible for me to cross her path by mistake.

I'd never see her again.

The realization hit me painfully in the chest. I'd already lost her twice, both because of my stupidity. But this one was different. In this instance, I was losing her entirely—as a friend and a lover.

What would I do then? I couldn't sleep outside her house anymore because she wouldn't be there. I couldn't keep her scarf any longer since it was just creepy. My entire world would be different, and the one girl I actually cared about would no longer be in it.

It actually scared me.

***

I walked into the house feeling weak. Marie's car wasn't in the driveway so I knew she wasn't there. Graduation was tomorrow and I hadn't seen her in a week. Every time I tried to run into her, it never worked. I always missed her—usually by minutes. Could I let her leave without saying goodbye? Could I really let her walk away without saying something?

"What's up?" Francesca's hair was in a ponytail and she wore sweatpants. The house was nearly empty because they took most of the furniture to the new apartment in the city. The place suddenly looked smaller, not bigger.

"I just wanted to see if you needed anything..." I looked around at the bare walls, trying to appreciate the last remaining essence of Marie. Soon I wouldn't be able to smell her perfume anymore. I wouldn't be able to see her stuff laying around the apartment, the things that reminded me of her.

"I'm good," Francesca said. "Just have a few more things."

"Great." Since there was no furniture I sat down and leaned against the wall. My knees were bent and my forearms rested on top. A heavy sigh escaped my lips, one full of depression.

Francesca stopped taping up the box then joined me on the floor. She sat on the carpet across from me, her legs crossed. "You okay?"

I shrugged and refused to make eye contact with her.

"Axel, if you want to say something to her, now is the time."

"And what would I say?" I looked out the back window into the back yard. The grass had grown a foot tall because the girls never mowed it. I would have done it for them but neither one of us had a lawn mower.

"The truth."

I didn't bother denying it.

"Axel, she's going to be gone by this weekend. In a new city with new people she's going to move on and you're going to miss your chance forever. If there's something you want to say, speak up."

"And what would I say?" I swallowed the lump in my throat. "That I don't want her to go?"

"That you love her and want to be with her."

I refused to look at her.

"Axel, how long are you going to lie to yourself? How long are you going to convince yourself that you're like Dad? You aren't."

I shook my head.

"Fine. Keep thinking that. But then you need to get over Marie and forget about her. End of conversation."

"I'll never forget about her..."

She rolled her eyes. "Then let it be. You love her so just admit it. It's written all over your face. It's written all over the walls. Marie got you to forgive Dad when I never could. She makes you happy. I can tell whenever you're together. She's made you into a better man. You couldn't keep it in your pants for a second before she came along, and now when you aren't even together you're faithful to her. Axel, this is the real deal."

I still couldn't admit it to myself.

"This is the bottom line, Axel. Can you live without her?"

Anytime I pictured the sky, it wasn't blue. When I pictured sharing my bed with anyone else, it made me more depressed than I've ever felt in my life. When I pictured my happiness, it was non-existent. I knew I would never care for another woman the way I cared about Marie. Whatever we had was special. It wasn't something that could develop with anyone else. "Yes...but I don't want to."

Francesca's eyes softened. "Then talk to her. She's still upset over what happened but if you say the right thing you could get her to let it go. You could get her to forgive you."

Would she ever forgive me after what I did? I didn't just hurt her once—but twice. "Why did she and Jason break up?"

Francesca was caught off guard by the change in subject. "He was tired of competing with you."

She told him how she felt about me?

Friday

"And they never slept together...if you were wondering."

That was a relief—the biggest one I've ever felt. It was wrong for me to feel that way after I hurt her so much, but it was the truth. I didn't want her to be with anyone but me.

"But that will change once she moves to New York. I can tell she's ready to push through and forget about you as quickly as possible. This is your last chance. Literally."

I was stuck at a crossroads and I wasn't sure which road to take. If I let her go, I'd return to my miserable existence in solitude. I'd always think about her no matter how much time had passed. I would wonder what she was doing, who she was seeing, and if she was happy. If I tried to make it work, I might get everything I wanted. But it also might blow up in my face.

"Axel?"

"Hmm?"

The front door opened and Marie walked inside. "That apartment is getting smaller and smaller with all the stuff we keep adding to it." She didn't notice where we were sitting because she was texting someone on her phone. She stood near the kitchen table and finished the message before she set her things down. "At least the view is nice." When she realized we were sitting on the ground, she tilted her head to the side. "Everything okay?"

Francesca turned to me, silently asking what I was going to do.

I still didn't know so I didn't react at all.

Francesca moved to her feet and grabbed her purse. "I need to go to the store...aspirin." She walked out and left us alone, the tension in the room increasing with every second.

She stared at me, her guard higher than a tower.

All my fears were still present. Anytime I loved someone I lost them. And if I had to lose Marie, I wouldn't know what to do with myself. But if I did nothing, I was losing her anyway.

I rose to my feet then closed the gap between us. When I was face-to-face with her like this, I noticed the distinct freckles on her face. They were hard to see under her makeup, but if I looked hard enough, they were there. The shape of her lips always caught my notice. They were plump and shaped in a sexy way. They felt even sexier when they were against my mouth. Her green eyes were unmistakably beautiful. I missed the way they used to look into mine—like I was someone worth looking at. "Do you have a minute?"

"Yes. But only one." She crossed her arms over her chest, keeping me at a distance.

Now that the hour had arrived, I was terrified. I hadn't thought this through or rehearsed what I was going to say. Telling someone your most personal feelings was a lot easier in theory. In reality, it was terrifying. One wrong sentence could ruin everything. "I'm sorry for all the things I've done to you. I'm sorry for the way I hurt you—more than once. I'm sorry I didn't treat you right."

Marie stared at me without any forgiveness.

"I wish I could take it all back."

"But you can't, Axel."

I tried to ignore her vicious demeanor. If I considered it too long, I would give up and walk out. "The first time we hooked up, it didn't mean anything to me. It was good sex with no effort. But after that, all I wanted to do was have you again. That's never happened to me before." It wasn't the most romantic thing to say, but it was the truth. "After that I got to know you better. I spent more time with you, and as those weeks passed, I didn't just want to be in bed with you. I wanted your affection, your words, and anything else you could offer me. I think even then...there was something there. But then I got scared.

"Every person I've loved has left. First, it was my parents. Then Francesca, the only thing I have left, almost met the same fate. My closest friend moved away to a different city. I've survived all of that, managed to find a reason to go on. But if I lost you, really lost you, I wouldn't be able to take a breath. I would be devastated beyond understanding. So, I thought keeping us at a distance would solve that problem. If I never really had you, I could never really lose you. It was less painful that way. But the entire time we've been apart...I've been miserable."

She kept her arms across her chest, but the fire died down in her eyes. She couldn't hold on to her anger—not forever.

"Now that you're leaving, really leaving, I know things will be different. I won't be able to see you whenever I want. I won't be able to use Francesca as an excuse to stop by and look at you. I won't be able to numb the pain in my heart by standing next to you. It just hit me now that I'm about to lose everything."

She kept her face stoic, her emotions hidden deep under the surface. She refused to lay down her cards until I laid mine down first.

Friday

"I don't want to lose you, Marie. I can't bare the idea of never seeing you again. I don't want you to move on with some other guy, and I don't want to go back to being with a different woman every weekend. You make me happier than I ever thought I could be and I don't want to lose that. So...please give me another chance. Please be with me."

She tightened her arms across her chest.

"I promise I'll be different this time. I promise I'm not going to get scared off and just leave. I'll be there for you. I'll be the boyfriend you deserve. After I get everything figured out I'll move to New York and we can be together—"

"No." She took a step back. "Axel, no."

The rejection stung—painfully.

"I'm tired of being flung around like a toy. Sometimes you want me and sometimes you don't. I'm not a dog. I'm a person with feelings. And I'm looking for a man who can treat me with respect. That's not you."

"I know I messed up in the past but I'll be different this time."

"You say that until there's a bump in the road. And then you're gone again. You're only saying this because you're scared. Your booty call is going to be in a different city so you can't just use her whenever you want. Axel, I'm not stupid. This has nothing to do with your feelings for me. You're just scared that things are changing."

"That's not true at all."

"History has a way of repeating itself." She looked away, staring at the empty living room. "You already played me twice. I always lose at this game I'm not rolling the dice anymore. I'm going to take my chances on someone else, a real man who can—"

"I love you." The words burned my throat on the way out. It was the first time I ever said that to someone besides family. It hurt, but in a good way. In the back of my mind, I knew how I felt about Marie. It'd been there for a long time, nearly from the beginning. I felt something special for her, something I couldn't feel for any other woman. She completed me, understood me, and she loved me. Anytime I pictured my wife's face, it was Marie. She was the future mother of my children, the woman I would grow old with and still make love to when we were gray. She was my forever.

She took a deep breath as her eyes softened, clearly not expecting me to say that.

"I've loved you for a long time, probably longer than you've loved me. I was just afraid to say it...but now I'm not. Please give me another chance to make this right, to be what you've always wanted." I put myself out there and now I was completely vulnerable. I revealed the true nature of my heart—that it only beat for her. I hadn't slept with anyone else because my body belonged to her exclusively. Even when I had the liberty of being with other women I didn't want to. All I wanted was her—from the beginning. "I know it took me a long time to finally get this right. I know I put you through months of torture, almost a year. But now I'm ready to be what we should have been in the first place."

Her arms slowly lowered to her sides until her hands were joined together in front of her waist. The anger that was in her eyes minutes ago was now completely gone. She no longer hated me, no longer resented me for the things I've done.

Now we could move forward and start over. She would move to New York and I would join her the second I found a job there. I'd drive up on the weekends to be with her until that time came. We'd have to spend some time apart but we would make it through.

"No."

I heard the words but didn't process them. My brain refused to. It was an answer I hadn't been anticipating, so therefore, it wasn't possible. She loved me. It was obvious in everything she did. She would forgive me. She had to. "What?"

"I'm sorry, Axel." Her eyes coated with tears. "I've already had my heart broken twice and I don't want to feel it a third time. Now I'm too scared to give this another chance—even if you do love me. Somewhere down the road you're going to get cold feet and leave again. I can see the ending before it even begins. I already went through it twice, and I'm not doing it anymore. My heart couldn't handle it."

Speechless, I stood there. I poured out my heart to her but it wasn't enough. I screwed up too many times. Now she couldn't trust me. She couldn't believe anything that came out of her mouth. I was a kid who cried wolf too many times.

"I'm not doing this to hurt you," she whispered. "I just don't believe in us anymore."

I looked at the ground because I couldn't stare at her anymore. She broke my heart right in half, severed it into two completely different pieces. Every breath I took pained me irrevocably. I'd never known this kind of anguish. I lost both of my parents in brutal ways and I almost lost my sister. But this...was a new level of heartbreak.

"I'm sorry, Axel. I'm ready to move on and start over." She walked back to the table and gathered her things. Even though this was her place, she took her stuff and walked out.

I stayed rooted to the spot, staring at the ground. The blood pounded in my ears, sounding like a distant drum. Now that the one thing I cared about walked out on me, I realized I had nothing. The loss washed over me like the freezing ocean in the middle of winter. If I just figured out my feelings sooner this could have been avoided. I wouldn't have lost something so precious—something vital to survival.

I was the only one to blame for this—and that made me feel even worse.

***

Despite how much pain I was in, I refused to miss my sister's graduation. Mom and Dad wouldn't be there so I had to be. Yaya was there, cheering Francesca on and being the best support in the world, but I knew I had a different significance to her.

I didn't want to look at Marie. Not because I hated her or never wanted to see her again. I just knew the longing would suffocate me. How could I be in the same area as she and not grab her and hold on forever? How would I keep my hands to myself? Even now, after everything we'd been through, I still considered her to be mine.

Francesca walked across the stage and received her diploma. Once she turned her tassel, I whistled and clapped. Yaya was screaming at the top of her lungs, proud of her only granddaughter.

Francesca didn't receive honors because she barely passed the semester, which was unfortunate. But she still made it through and that's what counted. Either way, I was proud of her.

A few minutes later, Marie walked across the stage. She looked like a drop of sunshine with her beautiful blonde hair and flawless skin. She sauntered to the president of the university and grabbed her diploma before she walked off again. Whistles erupted from the crowd, and I knew they were from men she didn't even know.

I clapped harder than everyone else.

"I'm going to hunt down Francesca," Yaya said. "I've got to get a picture."

"I think they're going to—"

Friday

Yaya was already gone, practically shoving the crowd aside.

I turned the other way and saw the graduates exit the end of the stage, coming back around to visit with their families. My eyes searched for Marie's face, not Francesca's. But I accidentally came across a face I didn't expect.

Hawke.

I narrowed my eyes and tried to determine if it was really him. He had the same hair, the same height, and the same type of clothes. He wore aviator sunglasses, the kind he usually wore on a sunny day.

It had to be him.

I pushed through the crowd to get closer to him, to need verification if it was really he. As I got closer the man turned to me. He stared at me for a few seconds before he turned on his heel and disappeared into the crowd.

"Hawke!" I peeked over everyone's head and tried to find him in the sea of families, but he was gone.

Was it really him?

"I did it!" Francesca ran up to me and hugged me. "I actually did it."

I forgot about Hawke and returned her embrace. "Congrats, Frankie."

She rested her face against my chest and squeezed me around the waist. "Thanks so much. I couldn't have done it without you."

"What are big and annoying brothers for?" I put on my best attitude since today was about her. I didn't want to be a stick in the mud because of Marie. I had tomorrow for that—and every day after that.

Yaya joined us. "How did you find her before me?"

I shrugged. "It's a sibling thing." *Or Hawke just led me to her.*

Yaya hugged Francesca so hard that Francesca gave out a squeak. "So proud of you, honey."

"Thanks, Yaya."

Yaya kissed her on each cheek. "I want to take lots of pictures."

"Good idea."

Marie walked over to us, her hair and makeup looking perfect. She was tall in her heels, several inches taller than she usually was. Up close she was even more beautiful. Staring at her actually hurt.

She looked at me with the same expression she gave me yesterday. There was pain there, like she didn't enjoy rejecting me at all. And if I looked hard enough I could still see the love behind her eyes. "Can you believe we're finally free of this place?"

"I know," Francesca said. "And we're off to New York."

"Can you take a picture of us, Yaya?" Marie asked.

"Good idea." Yaya pulled out her iPhone, something she still wasn't used to using. "Get closer together." She held the phone up and took the picture.

It was in that moment that I realized I might not see Marie again. And if I did, it wouldn't be for a very long time. The understanding was more painful than anything else. "Frankie, can you take a picture of us?" The only thing I had of Marie was her scarf, which I had no intention of returning. But I wanted something else, something I could actually look at.

"Sure..." She took my phone with a sad expression.

Marie stared at me in surprise.

I came to her side and stood there awkwardly for a second, wanting to touch her but unsure if I should. When I was this close to her, I could smell her perfume. I could see the way she was breathing. I could see the beautiful glow in her eyes. My arm hooked around her waist, resting naturally on her hip. I pulled her into my side, wishing I could do this every day. Her arm hooked around my waist and she smiled for the camera. I did the same.

Francesca took the picture and handed the phone back to me. "I got a good one."

"Thank you." It was hard to let her go, actually painful. I stepped away from her with a heavy heart, knowing I'd never be able to touch her again. I stuffed the phone into my pocket and planned on looking at the picture some other time. Now I had something I could treasure—for years to come.

Marie looked sad once the picture was taken. She couldn't force her happiness for even a moment. Guilt and pain were written all over her face. I never meant to hurt her on this special day, but at least I knew we felt the same way.

We were both miserable without each other.

Friday

CHAPTER TWENTY-TWO

Welcome To New York

Marie

"How was your first day?" Francesca was sitting at the kitchen table we had at our old place. It was way too big for the small apartment, and the chairs could barely fit next to it. She was looking over papers and maps.

"Great." I took off my jacket and set it over the back of the couch. My entire wardrobe was from Prada, and with my forty-five percent employee discount it was totally worth it. I was probably going to buy the stuff anyway. "Everyone at the office is so nice. And my office has a window that overlooks the city. It's a million times better than what I imagined."

"That's awesome." Francesca smiled.

"I'm actually excited to go back to work tomorrow."

"That'll wear off quickly—no matter how much you like it."

"How's the hunting?" She already started her search for a place to open her business.

"I found this building on the corner of fifth and Lexington. It's actually a really good spot, and the windows are absolutely perfect. So much natural light. It used to be a restaurant so it has the right floor plan. But if I get it I'll have to redo the back to make bigger kitchens."

"Let me see this place." I squeezed into the chair beside her.

"Here it is on the map." Francesca pointed at the red X she marked. "It's easy to reach by tourists and regulars and there's no competing business around it."

"Perfect."

"Here are some pictures." She handed me her phone.

I searched through the photos and knew the place would need a serious remodel. "It looks like it'll cost a lot of money to fix this place up."

"I know," she said with a sigh. "But the location is absolutely perfect. And I learned location is more important than anything else."

"True."

"And I know exactly how I want it to work. I just have to find a contractor who's willing to make my vision happen for a reasonable price."

"What's the cost of the lease?"

"Reasonable."

"How long do you have to decide?"

"A week."

"Well, do you have any other options?"

"A few." Francesca handed the papers over and allowed me to go through them. She sat there silently as I took my time, drumming her fingers against the tabletop. When the drumming increased in pace it was clear she was becoming impatient. "So...Axel is really a thing of the past?"

I didn't expect her to ask me that—at least right now. I was caught off guard. "Yeah."

"What happened between you two?"

She deduced enough. "He said he wanted to get back together but I said no. He hurt me too many times and I don't have any faith in him at this point. I just want to move on and find a guy who can get it right the first time."

Her fingers stopped drumming. "No offense, Marie, but romance doesn't work like that. There's no such thing as meeting a guy and getting it right on the first try. Relationships are complicated and take work."

"Well, they aren't as complicated as the thing I had with Axel."

"Probably not...but I don't think that's a good reason to not be with him."

I dropped the papers onto the desk. "Are you actually defending him?"

"No...yes." She shrugged. "I think he's an idiot who doesn't know his nose from his ass, but I know he loves you. He's been through a lot and it's hard for him to adjust to something like this. But the fact he finally got to that place should mean something."

I shook my head in disappointment. "He dragged me around for eight months."

"I know...but he didn't sleep with anyone else."

"That doesn't matter."

"It does," she argued. "That's not like Axel at all. He was faithful to you even though he wasn't committed to you. While he did some stupid things, he did a lot of sweet things too."

"Where is this coming from?" I asked. "You were on my side just a few weeks ago."

"I *am* on your side. And I think Axel could really make you happy if you gave him another chance."

I was tired of giving him chances. "If I did give him another chance, I already know what would happen. Down the road he would change his mind and back out again. He would get scared of something then take off. He's a flight risk and he'll always be a flight risk. I don't trust him, Frankie. That's the bottom line."

She turned away, giving up the argument.

"I know this is weird for you because he's your brother. He and I can be civil to one another if and when we are together. So don't worry about getting dragged into the middle of it. In a few months, it'll be like nothing ever happened."

"That's not what I'm worried about. I just want the both of you to be happy—and I think you need to be together to accomplish that."

"Drop it, Frankie." I wouldn't stop thinking about Axel until I stopped talking about him.

"Fine." She gathered her papers together and shoved them into her folder. "I'll figure this out later."

***

It took two weeks for me to become comfortable at the office. Eventually, the novelty of the building wore off and I grew tired of waking up at seven in the morning every day. But I was still happy with my job.

Axel was still in the back of my mind but it was easier not to think about him as often when I was in a new place. Nothing here reminded me of him so I was able to go about my day noticing new things for a change.

I joined a gym just around the corner from my office, and I found a coffee place on my way to work. The line usually wasn't very long and I could get my stuff quickly. The city was different than any other place I visited. It didn't matter what time of day it was, people were constantly coming and going.

I came home and set my things down.

"How was work?" Francesca just finished preparing dinner.

"Good." I released a sigh of exhaustion.

"Told you you would get sick of it." She placed the food on the table. It was tacos and rice.

"Yep. You called it." I kicked off my heels then joined her at the table. "So, how's the shop coming along?"

"I'm going to put my bid in tomorrow and hope I get it."

"Great," I said. "I hope you get the place."

"I do too."

"How do they decide?"

"They choose the business that's most likely to be successful."

"What does that matter?"

"Because a popular business means they can charge a higher rent. They get greedy with it."

I ate my tacos and drank my corona. Having Francesca there was nice because she cleaned the apartment, did the laundry, and had dinner on the table every day when I came home. It was like having a housewife—but without the sex. "How much do you think it's going to cost to renovate the place?"

She cringed. "A lot. I'll have to take out a loan—a big one."

"That's scary."

"I'll have to have someone cosign it because I don't have any collateral."

Axel.

"I'll figure out my next step after I get the business. No point in figuring that out now."

"You will get it, Frankie. The leasing owners will take one look at your business plan and know it's going to be a success."

"I hope so."

***

Friday

Since I was the one paying rent, I got the bedroom. Francesca slept on the couch. One perk for her was the TV. She could watch it before she went to sleep. I didn't have that luxury in my room.

Even though I was exhausted I couldn't get to sleep. I tossed and turned, feeling the cold sheets cling uncomfortably to my body. Every half hour I glanced at the time and realize what hour it was. Then I would groan and start the process all over again. The longer I couldn't fall asleep, the more anxious I became. It was a vicious cycle and didn't get me anywhere.

Then my phone rang.

No one would be calling me this late at night—except one person. But he had no reason to call me. I grabbed the phone and saw Axel's name on the screen. My heart surged into my throat and I could barely breathe. Just when I stopped thinking about him for a moment he crept back into my mind. I could just silence the call and try to go back to sleep but I didn't want to.

I wanted to answer the phone.

No good would come of it but I couldn't stop myself. I wanted it too much.

I took the call but didn't say anything. I just sat on the phone.

He didn't say anything either, knowing I answered.

I stared at the ceiling and felt the blood pound in my ears. It thudded painfully, diminishing my hearing.

"Hi..." His deep voice came over the line, masculine and beautiful. His hesitation was heavy, like he didn't know why he was calling at all.

"Hi..." My voice came out higher than I wanted it too. The emotion crept out against my will.

He fell silent again, saying nothing more.

I listened to his even breathing, knowing he was lying in bed just the way I was. Even though I left Myrtle Beach and rejected his advance, I still missed him. I missed him like crazy.

And I would always miss him.

I continued to listen to him breathe, taking comfort in the delicate sounds. My heartbeat synced with it, remembering all those nights we slept in each other's arms. I missed all his bedtime habits. If he were there now my sheets wouldn't be cold.

I pulled my teddy bear to my chest as I stayed on the line with him, wishing I were holding him instead of a stuffed animal. It wasn't clear why he was calling, but I suspected he didn't have a reason. He just gave into his desire and hit my name on the screen.

Just being on the phone with him made me feel better, made me miss him less. I tried to pretend he was beside me, sleeping alongside me just the way he used to.

"I miss you." His voice didn't shake but it possessed all of his need. The emotion was raw, palpable through the phone.

"I miss you too." I shouldn't have said that, but by the time I realized my mistake it was too late. Instinctively, I blurted out the words. My heart took the reins tonight.

After a long pause he spoke again. "How's Prada?"

"Good...I still like it."

"They're treating you right?"

"Yeah. I have my own office with a view, and there's usually lunch in the break room. I'll have to watch my weight."

"No, you won't. You're beautiful no matter how you look."

My heart skipped a beat.

"Are you liking the city?"

"Yeah. It's different but I like it so far."

"My sister isn't annoying you?"

"No," I said with a chuckle. "Never."

"Give it time."

I chuckled again.

He fell silent over the phone, listening to me breathe.

"How's everything?"

"It's okay." From the way he said it, it sounded terrible.

"Any luck on the job search?"

"I had a few interviews. One was in Florida. We'll see how it goes."

I wondered if he was looking to move to Florida so he could live as far away from me as possible. In a new place nothing would remind him of me.

"Are you seeing anyone…?" He asked the question hesitantly, like he shouldn't be asking it at all.

I hadn't been on a date with anyone, and I hadn't looked for a date either. New York was new and I was still acclimating to everything. "No."

His breathing increased slightly.

"You?" I wasn't sure why I asked the question when I already knew the answer.

"No. But I did tell Alexia off for that bullshit she said to you."

"Better late than never, right?"

Friday

"She's a psychopath. No wonder why her boyfriend dumped her."

I turned on my side and set the phone under my ear, listening to his presence over the phone.

"Are you doing okay? I'm always here if you need anything."

"I'm fine. Francesca and I can handle ourselves."

"How's her search for a bakery?"

I was surprised he didn't know this already. They clearly hadn't been speaking. "She thinks she's found the right spot. She's going to put a bid on it tomorrow and see what happens."

"Good for her. I hope she gets it."

"I'm sure she will. Good things happen to good people."

"True." Even though he had nothing else to say he stayed on the phone. He listened to my presence as I listened to his. "I'm sorry that I called you. I just miss talking to you. It's weird when I don't talk to you."

I felt my eyes well up with tears. "I know what you mean."

"I still drive by the house even though I know you aren't there."

I hugged the teddy bear to my chest.

"And I still have your scarf...it's in my top drawer."

I misplaced my red and green scarf and was never able to find it again. I thought when I packed up my things, I could find it again. Now I knew where it ended up. "I was wondering what happened to it."

"Now you don't need to wonder."

Talking to him was harder than I anticipated. My heart wanted to reach through the phone and touch him. My hands yearned for his body. I wanted to wrap my arms around him and never let go. The longing consumed me and blacked out everything else. "I should go..." I needed to get off the phone before I broke down and gave into my tears. The last thing I needed was for him to understand just how much I missed him, that walking away from him was the hardest thing I've ever had to do.

"I'm sorry for keeping you up. Good night, Marie."

"Good night, Axel."

Instead of hanging up he stayed on the line. His breathing was a distant sound, almost silent. "I love you."

His words echoed in my mind endlessly. I'd long to hear those words for so long, and now I've heard them twice. They were beautiful, but now they were beautiful in a painful way. They burned me, scarred me. Instead of bringing me joy they brought me pain. "I love you too."

CHAPTER TWENTY-THREE

Choices

Axel

I'd applied for positions all over the place. My focus used to be New York but now that Marie was there, I wasn't sure if that's where I wanted to be. Of course, I wanted to see her. I wanted to be close to her. But that might make things harder on me.

She didn't want me.

If I lived in the same city as her, bumped into her from time to time at Starbucks, I would never get over her. I would never move on and find happiness again. The best thing I could do for both of us was move somewhere far away.

I gave into my weakness and called her when I shouldn't have. I desperately needed to hear her voice, to listen to her breathe. I was going crazy without those sounds. Unable to sleep, I did the one thing that actually made me feel good.

Now another two weeks had passed and I was running on empty. I needed Marie to get through another day. The longing was swelling inside me, eating me alive. All I wanted was to hold her and end this suffering.

Sometimes I wondered if I could get her back if I tried harder. What if I say something to change her mind? What if I did something to make her reconsider? When I told her I loved her, she said it back. That had to mean there was some hope.

But if there were any hope would she have moved away? Would she have rejected my love? Was there really no hope at all and I was just seeing something that wasn't really there?

I didn't know.

After work I got a phone call that complicated things.

"Axel, this is Henry from Worldwide Investments. We met a few weeks ago."

I knew exactly who he was. He ran a huge investment company in Manhattan. It was one of the biggest firms in the city. Actually, in the nation. I applied in the expectation of getting rejected, so when they called me for an interview I was surprised. And when three weeks passed and I didn't hear from them, I just assumed they picked someone else for the job. "Hello, Henry. How are you?"

"I'm well. You?"

"Great," I said. "And even better because I expect this will be a good phone call."

He chuckled. "You're right, it is. We hired someone else for the position but they ended up being a poor fit for this company. It turns out, he lied about his transcripts."

What an idiot.

"I've already looked into your application and verified everything. Since you were our second choice, I'd like to offer you the job."

I wasn't even insulted at his use of words. I was second best but that didn't matter to me. Now I was at the front of the line. "Wow. That's great."

"So, you're still interested?"

I'd changed my plans to move back to Florida. I still had a lot of friends there from college. And the place didn't have a trace of Marie. I could get back into party mode and move on with other girls. But now that he was offering me the job of a lifetime, something I never expected to get this early in my career, I couldn't say no. It would be stupid to do so. "Absolutely."

"Great. When can you come in to discuss specifics?"

"I'm available whenever you are." I'd ditch work if I had to.

"How about tomorrow? I apologize for the rush, but we need you as soon as possible. Since the previous applicant didn't work out, we're short on time."

"That's fine. I can make it work." I'd prefer to put in my two weeks in at my current job because it was professional, but if I didn't have a choice they could deal with it. They were paying me shit anyway.

"Great. I look forward to seeing you."

"You too." After I hung up I fell on the couch and felt my body give way to the adrenaline. I just got my dream job and it literally fell into my lap. I was just about to pack up my things and move back to Florida when this opportunity fell into my hands.

It was like it was meant to happen.

***

Francesca spoke over the phone. "Hey, do you have a minute?"

I stood on the sidewalk near my parked car. People passed me, talking on their cell phones or drinking cups of coffee. "Yeah. What's up?" I hadn't spoken to her since she moved to New York. I was in a deep depression and didn't feel like talking to anyone, even family.

"I don't want to drop this on you but I don't know what else to do."

The seriousness of the conversation made me forget about my surroundings entirely. Whenever someone I loved was in trouble I was there—in a heartbeat. "What is it?"

"I got the bid for the bakery. But the cost of the renovations is insanely expensive. I qualify for a loan but I need someone to cosign it..." She understood exactly what she was asking me.

It was a big deal. If her shop went under I'd be stuck paying for it. It was terrifying. "I need to see your business plan before I agree to this."

"Okay." She didn't put up an argument. "Thank you, Axel."

"I didn't say yes."

"No. But I know you will."

***

Francesca was still living with Marie so I knew I would see her. That was one good thing about this situation. It'd been nearly a month since I set eyes on her. We spoke on the phone, but that was so long ago now that I was desperate for her presence all over again.

I knocked on the door and waited for Francesca to open it.

"Hey. You got here fast." She shut the door behind me and walked with me into the living room. The kitchen table was crammed against the window because there wasn't much room.

I glanced around hoping to see Marie, but she was nowhere in sight.

"And why are you dressed like that?"

I was wearing one of my designer suits. "I had a job interview."

"Seriously?" She sat at the table and stared at me with wide eyes. "That's exciting."

"And I got the job." I took the seat across from her.

"That's even better," she blurted. "Where?"

"Worldwide investments. It's the biggest firm in the city. When they offered it to me, I couldn't say no."

"Did you want to say no…?"

"I was planning on moving to Florida." I didn't need to explain why. Francesca would understand.

She nodded, a sad look in her eyes.

"But I couldn't turn it down so I'm going to look for a place."

"That's so exciting. I'm happy for you."

"Thanks."

"And I'm glad you aren't moving to Florida. That's too far away…"

"Like you'd miss me."

She looked me in the eye. "I would, actually."

Moments like these were rare. Sometimes I wasn't sure if they were real. "So…lay it on me."

She took a deep breath before she organized her papers. "If you say no, there're no hard feelings—at all. There's absolutely no pressure. I only asked you because—"

"You have no one else to ask."

She shrugged.

"So, all of this depends on me. No pressure at all…"

"Axel, if you say no, I'll figure out something else. There's always another way. I can work for a few years and save up some money. Honestly, it's not a big deal."

Friday

"Just get on with it."

She opened the folder and began her speech. It was clearly rehearsed and she was terrified I wouldn't approve of the model she spent so much time on. My sister didn't usually care for my opinion but she cared this time. I remained silent and listened to every word she said.

***

The front door opened. "I picked up Chinese."

"Thanks," Francesca said. "I love spring rolls." She just finished telling me her business model and was awaiting judgment.

When Marie spotted me at the kitchen table she dropped her bag of take out. "Shit."

I immediately got up and picked up the bag before anything spilled inside. Fortunately, I was wearing my best suit and did my hair to the best of my ability that day. I rose to my full height and looked down at her, mesmerized by the exquisite features of her face. She was absolutely beautiful—like always. I wanted to trace the lines of her lips with my tongue. Just the thought gave me shivers. "Hi..."

She took the bag with shaky hands. "Hi..."

"Sorry, I should have given you a heads up," Francesca said.

"Yeah, that would have been nice," Marie said sarcastically.

I looked her up and down, noting her designer clothes. "You look nice."

"Thanks." Her cheeks tinted slightly, showing she was nervous around me.

After four weeks apart, I thought I would be immune to her presence, but I suckered in all over again. My body burned with heat and my hands were freezing cold from not touching her. I felt the usual burn between us, trying to ignite.

Marie cleared her throat and walked around me. She placed the food on the table and gave Francesca a glare. "So...what are you guys doing?"

"I showed him my business model. I have to sign the loan tomorrow."

"Oh..." Marie nodded in understanding.

"Axel just got a job in the city," Francesca said. "It looks like he's moving here."

"Oh..." She took a deep breath like that was the worst news ever.

I put my hands in my pockets so I wouldn't grab her. "Frankie, I liked your model and think it has promise. But I need the evening to think it over."

Friday

"That's fine," Francesca said. "Take your time."

Now it was time for me to go but I didn't want to leave. I was only around Marie for a few minutes. I wanted more time with her. "Well, I'll talk to you later." I walked out, hoping Marie would follow me. When the door was shut behind me, I kept waiting for it to open again. For some reason I thought Marie might change her mind once she saw me. I knew she wanted me as much as I wanted her. I was still obsessed with her, still in love with her.

And I think she felt the same.

***

Since I was in the city, I met up with Hawke.

"You're moving here?" Hawke didn't hide his joy. "Dude, that's so awesome. It's just not the same without you being around."

"Yeah...I'm excited." *Not really.*

He finished his beer then watched me closely. "I have a feeling there's a bunch of shit going on in your life and I'm not sure if I want to hear about it."

"You don't."

He rubbed his chin with his fingers, his facial hair thicker than usual. "At least tell me you and Marie are still together."

"We broke up."

He cringed. "Come on, man."

"I was stupid and I screwed it up. When I tried to get her back again, she said we were done. She was tired of me yanking on her chain."

"Can't blame her…"

"So I lost her…again."

"Sorry, man."

I couldn't stop thinking about how her legs looked in that skirt. I couldn't stop picturing her soft hair and how it would feel against my lips. I missed her like crazy. "Now I don't know what to do. I'm moving here so I'll never get over her."

"Why would you want to get over her?"

"Did you not hear my story?"

"Do you love the girl or not?"

I'd told her how I felt twice. And the second time, she said it back. I never felt more alive than I did in that moment. "Yes."

"Does she feel the same way?"

I nodded. "She told me a few weeks ago."

"Then get her back, Axel. Turn on the charm and make it happen."

"It's not so simple…"

"What does that matter? If she's the one, don't let her go. Prove to her you're going to stick around. Make sure she knows you aren't going to go anywhere."

Even then, I wasn't sure of success.

"What other choice do you have?" he asked. "Sleep around and hope you feel that way again? Let me tell you from experience. You never feel that way more than once. It just doesn't happen."

I knew he was talking about Francesca but I didn't want to go any further down that road. "I'll think about it…"

Hawke dropped it when he knew I had enough.

I remembered the graduation and how I spotted him there. He turned and disappeared before I could get any closer. Even now, I still wasn't sure if I saw him. "Were you at the graduation?"

"What graduation?"

That was a dead giveaway that he was there. "Don't play stupid. You know Francesca just graduated. The fact you act like you don't know tells me you were there but you're throwing me off your trail."

He kept a stoic expression, like always. "I wasn't."

"Full of shit."

"Why would I go to her graduation?"

"Because you're the strangest dude I've ever known. That's why." He still checked on her and made sure she was okay even though they'd been broken up for a year. It didn't make any sense and never would.

"I'm not strange."

"Why won't you just admit you were there?"

"Because I wasn't?" he said like a smartass.

"Why are you lying to me?"

"How about we just drop this subject?" he said. "No good can come of it."

"Fine." Hawke was a different person when it came to Francesca. "How's work?"

"Really well. I left that old agency and started my own investment company."

"What?" *When did all of this happen?*

"I don't have an office or anything like that. I do everything from my phone, and meeting clients at Starbucks and stuff like that. But I've really made a good salary doing this. When I make money for my clients, they tell their friends, who then come to me. It's been snowballing, actually."

"Wow...that's really cool."

"Thanks. I like being my own boss. I hope it keeps progressing this way."

Friday

I wish I had that kind of drive. While I wanted to make money I wanted to work set hours then go home. I didn't want to carry the weight of a company on my shoulders. Stress and I didn't mix so well together. "Congratulations. Maybe you can open your own office someday."

"I think so. With the way things are going, I think I can make that happen this year."

Then he must be doing really well. Starting a business from nothing was a lot harder than people realized, and I'm sure Hawke worked night and day to make this happen. "I'll have to see it whenever it's ready."

"Maybe you could come work for me."

I laughed. "I'll pass. There's no way in hell I'm letting you be my boss."

He chuckled. "You're right. That would be a disaster, wouldn't it?"

"A big one."

He waved down the bartender and ordered another beer.

I was still on my first one and I didn't want to drink too much. I still had some thinking to do.

He cleared his throat before he asked his following question. "So...how's she doing?"

He asked about her every time we were together, so I wasn't surprised by the questions anymore. "She's doing really well. She's living with Marie now until she gets her own place."

He didn't seem surprised. It was like he already knew that. "Is she still seeing that guy?"

"Cameron? They broke up at the end of the semester. They're still friends."

He nodded and gripped the handle of his beer.

"She's been scouting a place to open her bakery and just landed a spot. Tomorrow she's going to sign the papers for the lease but the renovations are going to cost a fortune. She asked me to co-sign the loan. Her business model looks great but I'm still thinking about it. Without me, she has no one else. I'll probably do it regardless, but it's still a little frightening. If her place goes under, I'll be in debt for a long time." Francesca succeeded at anything she put her mind to, so there was a good chance the bakery would thrive. But there was always that possibility that it wouldn't.

Hawke's eyes narrowed on my face. "You have to co-sign?"

"Yeah. I guess her credit hasn't been built up enough."

He crossed his arms over his chest, his thoughts closed off.

"I'm sure it'll be fine but...you never know."

"Her business will flourish. Anything Francesca touches comes to life. I don't have a single doubt that it will succeed."

I wish I had that kind of faith.

He opened his satchel and pulled out a checkbook. "I want you to do something for me."

I eyed the checkbook with a raised eyebrow. "I'm not sure where this is going but I don't like it."

"I've made a lot of money this year—not to brag about it. And I want to help her."

"Please tell me this is a joke."

He clicked his pen and held it to the paper. "It's not. How much is it?"

"Hawke, you could lose everything."

"I won't. I know she'll do great."

"But you can't know that."

"I just do, man. We've got to make this happen for her. This is what she's meant to do."

I rubbed the back of my neck. "Even if I accepted your money, how would this work? I can't tell her where I got the money from and she knows I don't have huge lumps of cash laying around."

"This is what we're going to do. You're going to tell her you got a personal loan from the bank. She doesn't need to know it's from me. And since it's under your name, she needs to give you the money to pay it back. Then you give the money to me every month. If her business goes under, which it won't, she won't lose anything and neither will you. I'll take the hit."

Was he crazy? "We aren't doing this."

"We are."

"Even if her business is successful, it could take her twenty years to fully pay you back."

"And that's fine."

"It's a terrible investment on your part."

"I'm not investing for capital gain. I'm investing in her."

This was making even less sense. "Let me get this straight. You're willing to give Francesca hundreds of thousands of dollars to start her business even though she could fail and lose all your money, but you still don't want to be with her? Am I the only one who thinks that's the craziest shit I've ever heard?"

"Axel, drop it."

"No. I seriously don't get it."

"Then stop trying." He ripped the check out of the folder and slid it across the table. "Make it happen."

I stared at the check sitting on the table. "Once I hand this over I can never get it back. Do you understand that?"

"I do."

"If you ever need the money for an emergency, it's gone."

"I understand that as well. I would much rather see her use it than let it sit in my bank account."

I shook my head before I grabbed the check. "This is crazy..."

He shrugged. "I don't think it's that crazy."

"Because you *are* crazy."

**

I knocked on the door and came face-to-face with Francesca.

"You're still in the city?" She wore her pajamas with her hair in a messy bun.

"Yeah, I was meeting with a banker I know. I figured out a way to get you a loan without having to cosign it. The interest is a lot lower too."

"That's great," she said. "I guess I should have asked you to do that to begin with."

"But the loan has to be under my name. You'll give me the payment every month and I'll take care of it." This was the tricky part. Francesca may not go for it.

"But then you would totally be responsible if something bad happened…"

"I'm not worried about it. I know your business will succeed, and I'm making good money at my new job. It's not a big deal."

"Axel, it's not fair for you to take any kind of risk if you aren't making anything out of it."

"I wouldn't offer unless I was okay with this. So, please accept the offer."

She crossed her arms over her chest.

"Frankie, come on. It's the best interest rate and there's no co-sign nonsense. I really think this is the best way to go."

She still wasn't on board. She sucked her inner cheek.

"Well, I've already filed for the loan so it's done. You may as well just accept it."

"Axel…"

"It's not a big deal. I know your bakery is going to be awesome. Honestly, I'm not risking anything." These were Hawke's words, not mine. But I had to say them otherwise my actions wouldn't make any sense.

Friday

"Axel...that's so sweet. I don't even know what to say."

"You don't need to say anything. Let's just get that leased signed tomorrow so we can transform that place into the coolest bakery in all of Manhattan."

Her eyes flooded with tears and she fanned them to dissipate the moisture.

"Please don't cry." I rolled my eyes. "I really don't want to listen to it."

"Then let me hug you." She walked into my chest and hugged me tightly. "Thank you so much, Axel. No matter what happens I always feel you looking out for me."

I patted her back and stared into her apartment. Marie came into view, wearing leggings and a baggy sweater. Her hair was pulled back and her face was free of makeup. Even when she was dressed down she looked beautiful. I thought about Hawke's advice. He said I should try to win her back with everything I had. When I looked at her like this, that's all I wanted to do.

Because I couldn't picture my life without her for one more day.

CHAPTER TWENTY-FOUR

Date Night
Marie

I just closed down my office when Hawke called me.

How did he get my number?

He never called me before.

I turned in my chair until I was facing the floor-to-ceiling window. "What do you want this time?"

He chuckled into the phone. "It's nice to talk to you too."

"Francesca is fine. She's just working on her bakery. Nothing to report."

"Actually, there's something I want to talk about on that front. Can you meet?"

"Can't we just keep talking on the phone?" These heels were killing me and I was desperate to get them off. They may be beautiful and expensive, but they would claim my life eventually.

"No. This needs to happen in person. Can you meet me at that Italian Place on Twelfth and Broadway?"

I'd never been there before but I knew it was fancy. "Is it really that important?"

"Trust me. You'll want to hear what I have to say. I'll see you in thirty minutes." He hung up before I could get another word in.

He obviously knew Francesca had been living in the city for a while, and he knew she and I were living together. That guy had a way of keeping tabs on her without revealing his presence whatsoever. Maybe Hawke could leave the investment field and join the CIA.

***

I found his table near the window and took a seat. He was already there, wearing a suit and tie like he just got off work.

"It's nice to see you," he said politely. "You look beautiful, as always."

I sat down and placed my clutch on the surface. "You're such a suck up."

"I'm not the ass-kissing type. Well…I am. But in a different way." He winked at me.

"Ew."

"Let's get you a drink." He waved the waiter over and ordered a bottle of wine for the table.

"Is this a date?" I blurted, not understanding the candlelight, the wine, or the compliments.

"If you want it to be."

I didn't like this version of Hawke. He was strange. "What did you want to talk about?"

He glanced at the entryway then turned back to me. "First of all, how are you?"

"How am I?" I asked incredulously.

"Yeah."

"I've been better. I wish I was at home taking a hot shower." *Instead of sitting here listening to you.*

He nodded. "Yeah, I've had a hectic day myself. I started my own investment company and that's been pretty stressful. But I enjoy it, for the most part."

"Great, but I didn't ask."

Hawke hid any offense he felt. He talked me into coming here but he didn't seem to care about my opinion about anything. It didn't make any sense. "You still like working for Prada?"

"It's only been the first month. I would hope so."

He glanced at the entryway again.

"Are you waiting for someone?"

"No...just scoping the place out."

"Can we cut the shit and get to the point?" I asked. "Is there something you need to tell me about Francesca?" Hopefully, he wanted to get back together with her. But since so much time had passed I found that unlikely.

"Yes...Francesca." He nodded his head slowly. "There is something I want to talk about." His eyes darted to the entrance.

Hawke was the strong and silent type. It wasn't like him to talk so much and let his eyes wander at the same time. He was usually intense to the point of discomfort. "What are you playing at?"

Someone approached our table and stopped right next to me.

"Wow," Hawke said. "What a coincidence." He rose from his feet but left the chair out.

Axel stood there, looking just as confused as I was.

"Take a seat." Hawke grabbed him by the arm and forced him in the chair. "Well, I've got to run. Wall Street never sleeps. But how about you guys have dinner since the tab is already running?" He gave us a thumbs up before he walked off.

He totally tricked me into that.

Axel watched him go, the irritation in his eyes. "I swear, I had nothing to do with this." He wore a dark blue suit with a light blue tie. It looked perfect on him, fitting his broad shoulders and thin waist perfectly.

"I know." If Axel were lying I would have figured it out. Hawke played both of us. Now we were having a dinner neither one of us wanted. "He told me he needed to talk about Francesca."

"He told me the same thing."

"He got us good."

"Yeah, he did." Axel eyed the glass of wine on the table. "Did he drink this?"

"No." In fact, he didn't touch anything.

He grabbed it and took a drink. "Well, at least he ordered well."

I took a drink as well and was impressed.

Axel stared at me from across the table, his eyes moving over me in a gentle way. He used to stare at me like that all the time, like he could see all the way down into my soul.

I held his gaze until I was forced to look away. Sometimes that look reminded me of nights I tried to forget.

Friday

He grabbed his menu and took a peek. "Well, since this is an upscale place should we just order?"

I didn't want Hawke to win but I didn't want to be rude either. Hawke probably made reservations just to get us into this place. "Sure."

He handed me a menu. "I've never eaten here before but I've heard good things."

"Me too."

He opened his menu and browsed the selections. With his gaze averted, I looked at the nice features of his face. He just shaved so his jaw was clean. He had thin lips but they felt so full whenever I kissed him. His blue eyes reminded me of the ocean of a shallow cove. They were brighter than most blue eyes, unique in their brightness.

Before he looked up, I looked away.

The waiter arrived and took our order. Once he was gone, we had nothing else to do but look at each other. Being this close to him in a romantic setting was uncomfortable. It made me think of all the dates we went on, and what we did at the end of those dates. I missed the way his sweaty chest would rub against mine when we had great sex. And I missed the cuddling even more.

He seemed to be thinking the same thing but didn't feel any embarrassment for doing it. His arms rested on the armrests and he stared at me openly, like he'd be content if we didn't say a word to each other for the entire evening.

"How's work?" I wanted to change the tone of the evening. I'd already decided we weren't getting back together and I wasn't going to change my mind. Axel probably only wanted me because he couldn't have me.

"Good. I like it."

"Do they make you feel at home?"

"For the most part. I pretty much do my own thing with my own clients. There isn't a lot of interaction."

"Do you like that? Or dislike it?"

"I like it," he answered. "I talk to my clients enough. I don't need more conversation."

"What do you do?"

"The same thing as before. I make portfolios for clients and determine how we're going to invest their money. Worldwide is different though, considering it's a much larger company with a greater reputation. The clients invest money on a massive scale, so my returns and losses are much greater, and that can either help me or ruin me."

Friday

"Then it's more stressful."

"Yeah, I guess."

"How does the pay work? Is it commission based?"

"Yes and no. I have a base pay I receive no matter what my profits are. But I keep whatever I make on top of that."

Now that I picked his brain clean about his job I had nothing else to say. I wanted to keep this dinner as platonic as possible but I was running out of safe things to say. "I just wrote an article about the fashion show here in New York. That was a fun piece."

"Yeah, I read it. It was great."

He read it? "Oh..."

"I've read all of your articles. You're a magnificent writer."

Just when I thought that subject was safe it backfired. "Thanks..."

He continued to stare at me, looking deep into my eyes like there was nothing else he'd rather be doing.

I felt myself slip away and fall back into the hole I spent so much time crawling out of. When he told me he loved me, I said it back, which was a huge error. But now I was putting myself in a bad situation all over again. "What you did for Francesca was really sweet."

"That wasn't a big deal." He brushed it off like his actions were anything less than heroic.

"What are you talking about? You completely took all the risk."

"But she's going to make it. So there's no risk at all."

"And it's so sweet that you believe in her so much."

Axel rubbed the back of his neck, what he usually did when he was uncomfortable. "We're family. Families always stick together."

The fact he was being so humble about it made him more attractive. I always knew Axel had a big heart. He teased his sister a lot but he was always there when she needed him. "Well, I think what you did was incredible."

He grabbed his glass and took a deep drink.

I crossed my arms over my chest and hoped the waiter would return with our food soon. I wasn't hungry but I was eager for this dinner to end. It wasn't a good idea for Axel and me to sit this close together—ever.

Finally, the waiter brought our food and poured more wine into our glasses. I was relieved I had something to do other than stare at him and see him stare back. Axel made me comfortable on a dangerous level. If I let my guard down too far something would take a wrong turn.

He took a few bites of his food then looked at my plate. "How's your food?"

"Delicious. Yours?"

"Good. I'd eat this again." He ate with perfect manners, something he only did when he was in a public restaurant. Whenever it was just he and I he would leave his elbows on the table and even eat with his fingers.

I ate slowly and waited for the waiter to drop off the check. I had enough cash that I could slip it inside and we could go our separate ways. It was possible Axel asked Hawke to arrange this, but I had a feeling he didn't. "Hawke always sticks his nose where it doesn't belong..." He came all the way to Myrtle Beach just to get us back together. His attempt would have worked if that skank didn't answer the door and call Axel her boyfriend.

"What do you mean?"

Since Axel didn't know Hawke did that, and he didn't know about Hawke's other visits I realized my mistake in bringing it up. "I just find it strange that he did this..."

Axel shrugged. "He just wants me to be happy." He finished his food before I did. His plate was wiped clean because he ate every single bite.

"And being with me will make you happy?"

His gaze turned serious, his eyes and mouth falling in unison. "You and nothing else."

I quickly looked down at my plate so I didn't have to meet his gaze any longer. The muscles of my body were tightening all over the place. My heart was beating at a higher capacity than it could handle, and the unwanted heat flushed across my entire body.

The check arrived.

I quickly reached for it so I could slip the cash inside.

Axel got there first. "Nice try." He inserted the cash and set it at the opposite end of the table where I couldn't reach.

I wanted to object. If he paid, it made it seem like a date. But if I fought him for it we would be on this date even longer. It was best to leave now before I did something stupid. "I'm ready to go." I set my cloth napkin down then stood up.

Axel did the same, and he looked me up and down without being discreet. "You look beautiful."

Friday

I tucked my hair behind my ear. "Thanks." He said that to me nearly every time he saw me. Since it happened so often I didn't always know what to say except the obvious. "Thanks for dinner."

"My pleasure."

We walked out of the restaurant then stopped at the sidewalk. We faced each other to say goodbye. I was almost home free. All I had to do was say goodbye and it would be over. "I guess I'll see you later."

"I found a place." He acted like he didn't hear what I just said.

"An apartment?"

"Yeah. It's just a few blocks from here. I got lucky because a buddy of mine found it. Finding a good place in the city is nearly impossible."

"Good for you. I'm glad you got settled."

"Can I show it to you?" He put his hands in his pockets but he was still a threat. His beautiful blue eyes were impossible to resist. My favorite feature was his shoulders. They were broad and powerful. I used to grip them tightly while I rode him against the headboard.

"Uh..." I knew that was a terrible idea. I wasn't going to walk into his apartment alone. Something bad would happen because I wouldn't have the strength to control myself. Sleeping alone night after night was lonely as hell. It was even lonelier knowing I couldn't be with the man I loved. If backed into a corner I feared I would take the easy way out. "I really should be getting home. Francesca probably has dinner on the table."

"But you already ate."

"Yeah..." He had a good point. "But it's my turn to do the dishes."

"I'm sure you can do them later." He stood a step forward, silently pressuring me.

He wasn't this forward before. Last time we talked about our relationship he backed off and let me go. But now things seemed to be different. It seemed like I was prey and he was the predator. "Axel, it's just not a good idea. We shouldn't have had dinner to begin with."

"I promise I won't do anything," he said gently. "I just want to show you my place— that's all."

"Why do you want to show me so bad?"

He shrugged. "I thought we were friends. Don't friends do that sort of thing?"

"I guess. But you and I will never be friends."

It was the first time he showed the pain in his eyes. "Well, I'd like to change that. I'm just asking for a little bit of your time. I've promised I don't have a trick under my sleeve. I'm not going to kiss you."

"Promise?"

"I promise I won't even touch you."

Axel wouldn't break a promise to me so I knew his words were true. "In that case, I'd love to see it."

***

He gave me a tour of the whole place, showing me the kitchen, living room, and the two bedrooms. It was much bigger than the place I had with Francesca, and I had to admit I was a little jealous. "This place must cost a fortune."

"It's not cheap." He walked back into the living room, his hands still in his pockets. "But I wanted to have a nice place just in case I have clients over or something."

"They'll definitely be impressed." His furniture was black leather with clear countertops. It contained dark colors with a masculine aura. As soon as I walked inside I knew a bachelor lived here. Knowing he wouldn't make a move on me made me more at ease, but I still felt the prickle on the back of my neck.

He circled the living room and came back to me, stopping two feet away. "It's a few blocks from work so I can walk."

"That's nice. I walk to work every day. You can't beat that."

"No, you can't." He stared at me just the way he did at the restaurant. The intensity was returning to his eyes, his thoughts on my lips. His hands never left his pockets but his eyes were intrusive enough. "Thank you for coming by."

"Sure...no problem." My voice was suddenly weak and my body warm. Whenever he was close to me my mouth went dry. He had the innate ability to intimidate me with just a single look. Every power I had suddenly seemed irrelevant when it was dwarfed by his.

His eyes moved to my lips, examining every curve and the exact way they naturally parted. Without saying a word he told me what he wanted, that the phone conversation we had was still on his mind.

The only thing keeping me safe was that promise he made. "I should go..." Even though I said the words I didn't leave. My feet were stuck to the floor like roots of a tree.

"Marie, I don't want to move on. I don't want to waste my time trying to find someone else when there's only one woman I want. I may not have been there in the past, but I'm here now."

"You told me you wouldn't try anything—"

"I promised I wouldn't touch you. I'm not breaking that promise."

"You're still saying these things..."

"It's a free country, right? Free speech."

"Axel, I told you we were over—"

"We aren't over until we're no longer in love. Last time I checked, you were still in love with me. And I'm still in love with you. We have a chance to make this work. But you need to forgive me first."

"It's not about forgiveness. I just don't trust you."

"Then I'll make you trust me. But you need to give me a chance."

I wanted Axel with all my heart but I didn't want to go through that heartbreak again. He didn't just hurt me once, but twice. "I'm sorry..."

"Baby, come on. Now that I've lost you, I understand what I really want. I'm not going to mess this up again. I promise."

"Or maybe you just want me because you can't have me."

"That's not it." He said it calmly, like he'd already considered that possibility. He took a step closer to me.

Instinctively, I took a step back. I didn't want to be closer to him than I had to. If our proximity were too close, our flames would combine and create an explosion.

He took another step forward, forcing me back. Every time he came at me, I moved away. When my back hit the wall I realized there was nowhere else to go. I was cornered and unable to escape.

He took the final step and stood directly in front of me. Only mere inches separated us. He looked down into my face, his eyes studying my lips. Then he did something unexpected. He pulled off his jacket then tossed it on the floor behind him.

"What are you doing?"

With his eyes still glued to mine he removed his tie then unbuttoned his shirt. When each button came loose, more of his hard chest was revealed. He was nothing but muscle underneath his clothes. He had a chest made of concrete and abs of steel. He pulled the shirt off and tossed it aside along with everything else.

My tongue felt too big for my mouth, and my heart was too small to pump all the blood through my body. Perspiration formed on the back of my neck, sticking to the wall when I got too close.

He undid his belt and his slacks before he kicked them off. His dress shoes followed. Then he grabbed the top of his boxers, fingering them gently, before he pulled them off.

Instead of looking away like I should, I stared exactly where I shouldn't. His cock was long and hard, excited by the prospect of having me again that very night. He stood in just his socks, but he made those socks look sexy as hell. At six foot two he was all man. He rested his forearms against the wall on either side of my head before he leaned in, his face just inches from mine. He invaded my personal space without touching me.

Now I knew exactly what he was trying to do. He couldn't touch me but that didn't mean he couldn't seduce me in other ways. He was trying to get me to crack, to give into what we both wanted.

I needed to get out of there. "I have to go."

He didn't move.

I slid down to the floor then maneuvered awkwardly around him, trying not to touch anything or get something in my eye. On my hands and knees I crawled around him until I could get up again. Now that I wasn't directly next to him, I could get out.

But then I realized I was missing my clutch.

He leaned against the wall with it held in his grasp. Even though it was bright and pink, he made it look masculine. It contained my driver's license, money, and my phone. I couldn't leave without it. "Do you need this?"

"Yes." I held out my hand and refused to look at anything except his eyes.

"You can have it." He walked down the hall, taking it with him.

My eyes immediately went to his rock-hard ass. It was nice and tight, something worth taking a bite of. My body flushed with heat that reached all the way to my ears. He was successfully turning me on, and I hated him for that. "You can't take my stuff to keep me here." Even though it wasn't the best idea I followed him down the hall until I reached his bedroom.

He was lying on the bed with his head propped up on a few pillows. Gloriously naked and every woman's fantasy, he laid there like the perfect specimen for all men. My clutch lay across his chest while his arms lay on either side of him. "It's all yours."

Friday

I approached the bed with my arms across my chest. "This is pathetic."

"Pathetic that it's working?"

It was working but I refused to admit that. "What's tricking me into bed going to achieve? One night of sex and then I'm gone the next morning?"

"First of all, I'm not tricking you into doing anything. The act of sex is pretty distinct and there's no possibility you'll ever be tricked into doing it. Secondly, I don't want one night of sex where you're gone the next morning. I want sex with you every night—and I want you there every morning."

His sweet words loosened my resolve, and I hated that. "Just give it to me."

"Come get it, baby."

"You're ridiculous, you know that?"

"You're the one that keeps trying to get it."

I moved quickly like a snake and snatched it as quickly as possible.

But he was faster. He pulled it over his head where I couldn't reach it unless I crawled on top of him. "So close, baby."

"This is getting stupid." I crawled over the bed and his chest to snatch the clutch. If I had to touch him so be it. My knees rubbed against his hard skin, and even that simple touch lit me on fire. But I kept my head in the game and went for the clutch.

Axel grabbed me by the shoulder and rolled me underneath him, pinning me down so I couldn't get away.

"What the hell? You promised you wouldn't touch me."

"But you touched me first, and that broke the promise. How can I not touch you if you're touching me?"

"You're an ass." I tried to kick him off but I couldn't.

He pressed his face close to mine then dug one hand into my hair. "If you want me to get up all you have to do is ask." He grabbed the clutch from my hand and tossed it on the ground. "Just ask." He brushed his nose against mine before his lips trailed to my jawline. He kissed the skin gently then moved to my neck. His kisses were sensual rather than aggressive. His body told me he wanted to rip off my clothes and have me then and there, but his kiss said otherwise. "Can I undress you?" He looked into my eyes and waited for the answer.

I was a goner. "Yeah…"

He peeled my clothes away, kissing every inch of my body as it was exposed. He removed my skirt and then everything else, stripping me until I was completely naked underneath him. Then his lips traveled between my legs, giving me the kind of kiss that made women scream.

I arched my back and gripped his headboard as he did amazing things to me. He circled my clitoris with his tongue then sucked the area aggressively. I panted loudly and let out a few moans. Everything he was doing felt out of this world. I hadn't had sex in nearly two months and I was going crazy. Axel gave me exactly what I'd been longing for.

When he brought me to a climax, I screamed his name so loud I feared his neighbors would hear and complain the first chance they got. He lit a stick of dynamite and let it explode inside me, burning me from the inside out in the greatest way possible.

My vision blurred and all I felt was unbridled pleasure. I could see the heavens and the stars and everything else. I drifted away like a feather on the wind until I slowly came back to earth, my body relaxing.

Axel crawled up the bed and lay next to me, his lips coated with my moisture. Instead of moving on top of me and getting ready for the grand finale, he turned off his bedside lamp and brought his bedroom into darkness.

"What are you doing?"

He wrapped my leg around his waist and pulled us close together. His hand moved up my back and rested between my shoulder blades, a few strands of hair trapped underneath. "Going to sleep."

"You went through all that trouble to seduce me and you aren't going to get off?"

"I didn't seduce you to get sex. I seduced you so I could get you to sleep with me."

"Then why did you go down on me?"

"I didn't want to get you hot and bothered and not finish the job."

This entire time I thought I had him figured out, but in reality I didn't have a clue. He played me, and he played me well. "All you want is to sleep with me?"

He nodded. "It's my favorite thing. Every night when I go to bed I wish you were with me." His lips moved to my forehead where he pressed a single kiss. "I used to have it every night until I threw it away. Now I spend every night tossing and turning, lost in the nightmares you used to keep away. I had the most beautiful thing in the world and I screwed it up. I'll never take you for granted again—if you give me another chance."

When he said pretty things like that it was impossible for me to remain strong. I couldn't keep him away, and my body no longer responded to my commands. His bed was comfortable and he was even more comfortable. I wanted to stay like that forever—with him.

***

When I woke up the next morning, I realized what I'd done. Now I was back to square one. I was trapped tightly around his finger, playing right into his game. If I wasn't careful I'd be in the same position I was before. My heart would beat only for his, and when he turned around and took off I'd break into pieces.

I slipped out of the bed and changed as quietly as possible. Axel didn't stir, his position exactly the same as before. It was some unearthly hour that no one should be awake to witness. I grabbed my clutch and carried my heels to the front door. My hair was a mess and so was my makeup.

Then I realized I never told Francesca where I was last night. She was probably freaking out. I pulled out my cell phone from the clutch and looked at my messages. Like I expected, she tried to check up on me more than once. When I got to her last message I realized she already figured it out.

Axel told me you're spending the night. We'll have to talk about that when you get home...

I growled then shoved the phone back into the clutch. Then I got out of there as quickly as possible, not wanting Axel to wake up and try and prevent my escape.

***

To my surprise, Francesca was awake when I entered the apartment.

She was sitting at the kitchen table going over the blueprints to the bakery. They'd already begun construction of the little shop, and in just a few weeks it would be ready to open. "Spill it."

"I need a date—tonight." I needed to find a guy and move on without looking back. The only thing that could get Axel off my back was another man. When Jason was around, Axel respected his significance to me.

"Wait, what?" She turned around and looked at me, her hair in a messy bun and her eyes still drooping with sleep. "What the hell happened over there?"

"Axel is done. I'm done with him."

"Ugh...then why did you sleep there?"

"Because he tricked me."

"He tricked you into falling asleep?"

"It's complicated," I argued. "All I know is, I need to move on right now. Otherwise, he's going to keep chasing me."

"Did you sleep with him? Like, you know?"

"We just fooled around. He said he didn't want to have sex—just to sleep with me."

"Awe..."

I'd never heard Francesca utter that word about Axel. "Don't let him drag you down."

"Come on, Marie. I've never seen Axel work this hard for anything in his life. I think he's finally got his head on straight and he's ready to have the relationship you want."

"Or that's just what he thinks. Once he has me and he gets bored he'll take off again."

She rolled her eyes. "He never took off because he was bored. He left because he convinced himself he didn't love you. But we both know that was just a defense mechanism over all the people he's lost. Now that you helped him confront those feelings, everything should be fine."

"That's what you think...but who really knows."

Francesca gave me an irritated look. "Now you're doing the exact same thing he was. You're trying to find any reason not to be with him because he hurt you."

"Can you blame me?"

"I just think you should both let go of the past and just be together."

"It's more complicated than that."

"Well, I think—"

"Frankie, I don't care what you think. This is my problem and not yours. I'm going to find a date tonight and I'm moving on for good." I marched down the hall so I wouldn't have to see the pissed look on her face. I knew I ticked her off but I didn't care at the moment. I didn't care about anything.

Friday

CHAPTER TWENTY-FIVE

Slip Away

Axel

When I woke up the next morning, she was gone.

She slipped out of my grasp and left the apartment without locking the door behind her. Since I was already running late to my new job I didn't have time to call her and confront her about it. I didn't like waking up alone. It made it seem like last night meant nothing to either one of us.

Which wasn't true.

I got to work just on time to meet with a new client. Since my day was booked with back-to-back appointments I didn't have a chance to call Marie. I wanted to talk about last night, to make sure she wasn't running from me.

Hawke's words made a lot of sense, in retrospect. If I loved this woman and wanted to be with her, I had to make it right. I couldn't just let her go. If I did, she would eventually get over me and end up with someone else.

I should end up with her.

I'd been with a lot of women in my lifetime. When I lived in Florida all I did was party, get laid, and study. My time there accumulated into a lot of sex so I had a lot of experience. I think that's why Marie meant so much to me. She was the first woman I wanted to sleep with more than once.

Didn't that mean something?

I didn't think about marriage and kids. In fact, it never crossed my mind. But with Marie I could picture a future—one that I wanted. I could see myself spending my life with her. I could picture her having my children. These thoughts had never entered my brain before.

So, I should listen to my instincts.

I had to get her back. I wasn't sure how I was going to manage it but I would figure out a way.

***

Just when I got ready to call Marie, Francesca's message popped on the screen.

Marie is being a brat. She found some guy online and now she's going on a date.

What the hell? How did she pull that off so quickly?

Don't tell her I told you.

This conversation wasn't meant for texting. I called her and listened to her pick up on the first ring. "She has a date? With who?"

"I don't know. He just picked her up and they left."

Damn, she didn't waste any time. "This is a nightmare."

"Tell me about it. She's so determined to move on from you that she's being stupid."

"Very." I stood outside my building with my hand in my pocket. I thought sleeping together would fix everything. Whenever we were together all the pain disappeared. But she was clearly holding a grudge. "Where did they go?"

"That Thai place next to her office."

I was new to the city but I think I knew what she was talking about.

"But you shouldn't intervene. I'm just telling you so you have a heads up."

"Then what am I supposed to do? Let her finish her date then talk to her?" I wasn't letting some chump touch my girl.

"I don't know but barging in on their date will probably make it worse."

Friday

I growled into the phone and started to pace. "Frankie, what do I do? Doing nothing isn't an option."

"I don't know...you'll have to mess up the date without actually messing it up, you know?"

"No," I snapped.

"What if you just bump into her and take it from there?"

"I guess I can do that..." I just didn't know what I was going to do once I got there. "Why are you helping me anyway?"

"Because Marie is being a poopy head and I'm tired of it."

"A poopy head?"

"If she really didn't want to be with you anymore, I'd let it go. But it's so obvious she's still in love with you. Not being with someone simply out of principle is ridiculous."

At least she was on my side.

"So, are you going to head to the restaurant? They're probably there by now."

"Yeah..." I sighed into the phone. "Wish me luck."

"Good luck..." There wasn't an ounce of belief in her voice.

***

I walked into the restaurant and located their table near the back. Marie was still in her work clothes but she looked stunning, like always. But she would look stunning in a beekeepers suit.

I adjusted my tie and prepared myself for the conversation. The shit would hit the fan and Marie would probably be more pissed off at me but I had to do something. I hurt Marie several times and I deserved this. But I wanted the torture to end.

I walked to their table, trying to appear as calm as possible.

Marie spotted my approach, and once she saw me her eyes lit up in flames. She wanted to murder me right then and there.

I kept going and stopped when I reached their table. To my misfortune, her date was a good-looking guy. He was built like he threw tree logs around for fun, and his suit told me he did something impressive for work.

Marie wanted to kill me. Like, actually kill me.

Her date stared at me hesitantly, like he wasn't sure if I were a waiter or a friend.

Marie refused to speak. Instead, she silently threatened me.

Friday

Now that I was there, I didn't know what to do. Marie was scaring me a little bit, and I wasn't sure if I could take her date if I had to. Somehow, I had to ruin this date without actually ruining it.

How did I accomplish that?

Then I got an idea. I didn't like the idea very much. In fact, it made me sick a little bit. But desperate times called for desperate measures. "Oh my god, hi." My voice came out high-pitched and over enthused. "It's so nice to see you here. I just left Prada and thought I'd stop by for dinner."

Marie's anger immediately disappeared. I'd never seen her look so bewildered.

"Who's your cute friend?" I took a step toward her date and gave him a smile.

He immediately stiffened. "Charles."

"It's so nice to meet you, Charles." I rested my hand on his shoulder and gave it a squeeze.

He tensed again but didn't push it away.

"You guys wouldn't mind if I joined you, right?" I took the seat next to Charles and scooted my chair close to him.

Marie was mortified. Her cheeks were turning red and she tried covering her face.

"So…you've got a boyfriend?" I'd only do this for one person. If Marie weren't the love of my life, I wouldn't be caught dead doing this. But there was no other way I could chase him off.

"I'm straight, actually." He nodded to Marie. "Hence, why we're on a date."

"Oh…I see." I sighed in disappointment. "But how do you really know what your preferences are until you try everything?" I scooted closer to him, my thigh touching his.

He immediately moved away, uncomfortable.

Marie's face was getting redder by the second.

"You know who you remind me of?"

He kept his eyes glued to his menu.

"One of the guys at Chippendales. He's so fine." *How long did I have to push him until he cracked?*

Marie finally recovered enough to speak. "Axel, if you don't mind we'd like to be alone."

"Oh, come on." I placed my hand on his wrist. "I'm just being nice."

He pulled his hand away violently. "Marie, I have somewhere to be. Maybe we can get together another time." He stood up and buttoned his suit before he marched off, the sway of his shoulders showing his anger.

My plan worked.

Marie turned on me. "What the hell?"

I scooted into his vacated chair and returned my voice to normal. "What the hell to you? I wake up and you're gone?"

"Last night was a mistake."

"How? We didn't do anything."

"It just was," she snapped. "We're never getting back together so you need to drop it."

"I'm not dropping it until you give me another chance."

"You only want me because you can't have me." Her voice rose until other tables could hear us.

"No. I want you because I know I'm supposed to marry you."

Her eyes widened to their full capacity and she stopped breathing.

Now I wasn't afraid to say things like that. I was terrified of my relationship with Marie because I knew how much she meant to me, even in the beginning. She had the power to destroy me. I could detect it long ago. But now I wasn't scared of it. In fact, I was scared of losing it. "I'm supposed to be with you for the rest of my life. That's what's meant to happen."

"Meant to happen?" Her voice came out as a whisper, no longer a shout like it was before.

"I'm not saying I believe in destiny or soul mates like Francesca does. But I know you're the one for me. You're the only woman who's ever made me feel like this. And not to sound like an ass, but I've been with a lot of them. From the beginning I knew there was something special here. The first time we slept together, I couldn't stop thinking about you. And every time I was around you my heart was in overdrive. I'm sorry I screwed this up so many times, but the only reason why I pushed you away was because I was scared. I was scared of losing the woman I loved, so it was easier not to lose you to begin with. But now that I understand what my life is like without you, I realize it's better to love and lost than to never love at all." When she did nothing but stare at me, I knew I was getting through to her. "Marie, please give me one more chance. I'm here now and I'm ready to give you whatever you want. I'll be the best damn boyfriend of the year. I'll be there, every day. Every morning when you wake up I'll be beside you. And every time you tell me you love me I'll say it back." I bared my entire soul and now it was out in the open. I just set myself up for success or failure. I wanted this woman so desperately that I risked my own neck just to make it happen. In my heart, I knew she was supposed to be mine. And if I lost her forever I would always regret it. When she didn't say anything for several moments I grew tense. "Marie?"

She continued to stare at me passively, her eyes not giving anything away. Her breathing had increased. Her chest rose and fell at a heavy rate. Her hands were under the table so I couldn't see them but I suspected they were fidgeting together.

"Baby, I'm asking for one more chance. That's it."

She remained silent.

If I lost her, I wouldn't know what to do. I couldn't go back to my previous lifestyle of meaningless sex with strangers. I couldn't be with anyone else but her. My existence would be hollow and empty.

"I love you."

My heart skipped a beat when I heard those beautiful words. Quiet conversations continued around us at the different tables. To onlookers it seemed like we were having an ordinary conversation. But in reality, our whole world was changing. She'd never said those words to me before and I said them back. Now was my chance. "I love you too."

Her eyes watered but the tears didn't fall. Her chest continued to rise and fall at a rapid rate. She was in public so she tried to keep her emotions in check but it was becoming progressively harder.

I leaned over the table so we were as close as possible. "One more chance?" I extended my hand to her, my knuckles resting on the surface.

She stared at it for nearly a minute before she gently placed her hand on top. "Yes."

She said yes.

I couldn't believe it.

I did it. Somehow, I did it.

Marie was mine.

I brought her hand to my lips and kissed it. "I won't hurt you again. I promise."

She nodded.

I continued to hold her knuckles against my mouth as I stared at her. "Will you have dinner with me?"

She cleared her throat, dissipating the emotion. "Since we're here…"

"It'll be our first date—our last first date."

***

Friday

Without discussing it, we went to my apartment. Everything was exactly the same as it was when she came over the night before. Even though I hadn't had sex in nearly two months I wasn't eager to get some action.

I just wanted to be with her.

Once the door was shut and we were alone, I cupped her face and gave her a slow kiss. It felt so good to feel her mouth against mine. The softness of her lips were unparalleled by anything else I've ever felt. My arms tightened around her and I deepened the kiss, pressing her against the wall. My hand dug into her hair automatically and I grabbed a fistful of hair. I loved gripping her this way, making her mine.

Her hands moved to my shirt where she unbuttoned it from top to bottom. Her fingertips moved over my skin slowly, taking her time as she got me down to my bare skin.

Slowly, we moved to the bedroom, a trail of clothes developing behind us. I saw her naked last night, but I was eager to see her again. This time, she was really mine. After we made love and went to bed, she would be there the following morning. That was the most exciting part of all.

I got her on my bed, her legs already wrapped around my waist. My socks were still on but I didn't care enough to take them off. She didn't seem to care either. When I looked down at her, I didn't see a hot blonde with big tits. I saw a beautiful woman I wanted to cherish forever. Never in my life had I been the romantic type but now I was—with Marie.

My cock found her entrance like it always did, and I gently pressed inside her, stretching her like I had a hundred times. Instead of kissing her, I watched her reaction. The way she used to look at me had returned. There was nothing but love in her eyes, treasuring me as well as the moment.

I loved being inside her. There were no words to describe how it felt. Not only was it pleasurable, but it was meaningful. I was the only man to have her this way, and I would be the only man to have her this way. I wanted to spend the rest of my nights like this, being with one woman. A year ago I wouldn't have been able to fathom this moment. But now I couldn't picture my life being any different.

She rocked with me on the bed. "I love you." Her fingers dug into my hair and she cradled my face close to hers. Her lips were parted from her heavy breathing. When she

Friday

said those words they were innately sexy, better than any dirty talk I'd ever had.

"I love you too, baby."

***

Hand-in-hand, we walked inside Marie's apartment.

Francesca was watching TV on the couch, and when she heard us walk inside she turned around. "Hey, where were you—" She stopped in mid-sentence when she saw our joined hands. "About fucking time." She left the couch and walked over to us. "I thought this day would never come."

I wrapped my arm around Marie's waist. "We just came by to get her things. She's staying with me for the week."

"Cool," Francesca said. "I get the apartment all to myself without having to pay for it. I feel like a housewife in the fifties."

"Just keep the place clean." Marie walked into her bedroom and started to pack her things.

I eyed her ass until it was no longer in view.

"So, how'd you do it?"

I turned back to Francesca. "Do what?"

"Remove the guy."

"Oh…I came on to him."

324

Her eyes narrowed.

"I acted gay for a few moments. It worked like a charm."

"I think you were supposed to fight for her. You know, do something romantic."

"Well, the guy was huge. Hitting on him was a lot easier."

Francesca covered her mouth and tried not to laugh. "Then what happened?"

"I told her how I felt...didn't hold anything back."

"Which was...?"

"You're nosy, you know that?"

"Look, if you don't tell me Marie will."

Sometimes I forgot they were best friends. "She's the one." That was all I needed to say.

Francesca grinned from ear-to-ear. "Awe..."

I rolled my eyes.

"You're going to married, aren't you?"

I shrugged. "Not today. But someday."

"Awe..." She clapped her hands again. "Marie is going to be my sister-in-law. Oh my god, I'll be her baby's aunt."

"Let's not get carried away. She's just spending the week with me, for now."

"Whatever," she said. "I'm going to start collecting bridal magazines and putting pictures together...it's going to be great."

"Whatever."

Marie returned with a bag over her shoulder. "I think I got everything."

I took it from her. "Let's go. We've got a lot to catch up on."

"Awe." Francesca clutched her hands to her chest.

"Shut up already." I opened the door and walked out.

Marie hugged Francesca. "I guess I'll see you when I get back."

"Have fun." Francesca pulled away then squeezed Marie's wrists. "I want the scoop when you get back."

"You got it."

I grabbed Marie's hand and pulled her out before Francesca invited herself to come along. Those two were inseparable, and I needed to get them apart before Marie invited her along.

***

Instead of watching the movie we made out on the couch. She straddled my hips with her arms around my neck. She kissed me hard on the mouth, giving her tongue before her lips again.

My hands had yanked up her skirt and now gripped her bare ass. My cock was hard and rubbed against her panties through my slacks. With my head resting against the back of the couch I kissed her like a horny teenager. Kissing was still my favorite thing to do.

The alarm over the oven started to beep.

Marie pulled away, her lips puckered and red. "Chicken is done."

I didn't care about food at the moment.

She got off my lap and fixed her skirt, hiding her beautiful ass from view. Then she disappeared into the kitchen and checked on the food.

I eyed my keys and wallet on the table before I stood up and opened the front door.

"Where are you going?" Marie called from the kitchen.

"Nowhere, baby." I pulled up the rug and grabbed the spare key from under the mat. I shut the door again then walked into the kitchen.

Marie just finished preparing the dinner plates when I walked in.

"I want you to have this." I held up the spare key. "Come and go as you please." I wanted her to be at my place all the time. Whenever I got off work I had to pick her up first then take her to my apartment since she couldn't get inside on her own. Now she could sleep in late when I went to work and lock up before she left. If she ever wanted to come over for no reason at all, she could just walk inside.

A slow smile crept over her lips. "You're giving me a key to your place?"

"Yes." I placed it in her hand before I closed her fingers around it.

"You're sure?"

"Absolutely." I'd ask her to move in if it weren't too soon.

She placed the key on the counter. "Thank you. I'd give you mine but—"

"I don't want it." Not when Francesca was still living there. I never wanted to walk in when she didn't know I was coming.

Marie gripped the front of my shirt and pulled me in for a kiss. "Thank you. That was sweet of you."

"I'm a sweet guy." *For her.*

The doorbell rang and shattered the moment.

She eyed me with a raised eyebrow. "Expecting anyone?"

"No." No one even knew I lived here. "It's probably a girl scout or something." I walked to the door then peeked through the peephole. To my surprise, Hawke was on the other side.

I opened the door. "Hey, what are you doing here?"

"Hello to you too. You invited me to come by and check out your place."

"I did?" I didn't remember that. "When?"

"A few weeks ago. I just didn't have time until now." He spotted Marie over my shoulder, and a slow grin stretched his face. "Looks like you're busy..."

"Uh, yeah." Now I was grinning.

He clapped me on the shoulder. "Good for you, man. Let's meet up for a beer tomorrow—if you're free."

"Yeah, I'll text you."

Hawke waved over my shoulder. "Nice to see you, Marie."

"You too," she said with a smile.

I shut the door then came back to her. "He was rooting for us as much as Francesca was."

"It's sweet." She finished dinner then handed me a plate. "Our best friends want us to be happy. And in my book, that makes them good friends."

Friday

***

"I haven't been to my apartment all week. I need to go." She had her bag over her shoulder with a remorseful expression on her face. Every time she tried to reach for the door, I stopped her.

"Stay." I kept grabbing her and pulling her back into me. Our week together passed within the blink of an eye. I remembered every single moment with her, but somehow the time passed in a crazy blur.

"I have no clothes."

"Wear mine."

She rolled her eyes. "I can't wear men's clothes to work."

"You'll make them look sexy."

"And none of your stuff is Prada."

"They'd really fire you for that?" I gripped the small of her back, wanting her back in my bed.

"I haven't seen Francesca in a week. I need to check on her."

"She's fine." *And if she wasn't, who cares?*

"I'm out of underwear."

"You don't need them anyway." My hand moved up her skirt until I touched her cheeks.

She slapped my arm playfully. "I'll see you soon, okay?"

E. L. Todd

"You'll be back in a few hours?" Could I really survive a few hours without her?

"I was thinking maybe tomorrow night."

"What?" I blurted. "That's too long."

"I can't just abandon Francesca and my apartment."

"Then I'll come over."

She cringed. "That apartment is too small as it is. We can go a night apart."

"Speak for yourself..."

She cupped my face and gave me a slow kiss. "Have a guys' night. Do something with Hawke."

"Hawke isn't sexy like you are."

"I would hope not."

"And his dick gets in the way."

She rolled her eyes. "Well, just use your imagination." She kissed me on the cheek before she walked out.

Ugh. I felt dead inside the second she left my arms. I was always smitten with her but now I realized I was purely obsessed. "Text me when you get home." I peeked my head out the door and watched her walk down the hallway.

She kept walking but glanced over her shoulder. "Okay."

"And text me before you go to bed."

"Maybe. Maybe not."

Friday

***

Hawke and I met at a sports bar to watch the basketball game.

"So...how long are you going to make me wait?" His eyes were on the TV.

"You buy me a beer and think you're going to get some action?"

He grinned. "What happened with Marie?"

"I took your advice and hunted her down."

"That doesn't sound romantic...sounds scary."

"You know what I mean. I didn't give up."

"Good for you." He took a drink of his beer. "I'm surprised you aren't with her now."

"I would be if she didn't go home. She said she wanted to spend time with Francesca, some crap like that."

"I see how it is," he said with a chuckle. "You're with me because you have nothing else to do."

"Hey, cut me some slack. I'm in love. When you're in love that person is all you think about. It's like, I breathe just so I can survive to see her again. I wouldn't expect you to understand."

The atmosphere suddenly grew tense.

I realized my mistake. "Sorry..."

"It's okay," he said. "I know exactly what you mean."

I stared into my beer because I still felt foolish for what I said.

"I'm happy for you, man."

"Thanks..."

He clanked his beer against mine. "Enjoy every moment."

"I will."

He watched the game for a few minutes before he circled back to his favorite subject. "How is she?" He almost never referred to her by name.

"She's good. Waiting for the remodel to be finished."

"She didn't raise any questions about the money?"

"I told her it was all me. I felt deceitful taking all the credit, but Marie thought it was sweet."

He chuckled. "Maybe I helped you get back together."

"You already did with that dinner you arranged."

"What can I say? I'm a matchmaker."

I pulled my phone out of my pocket and set it on the table. If Marie texted me, I would know about it immediately. "Anyone special in your life?" Hawke used to tell me about the girls that visited his bed. He would go into detail about it, but after Francesca came into his life he didn't tell me anything.

"There's never anyone special."

"You know...just because it didn't work out with Francesca doesn't mean you can't tell me things." It was awkward but we had to move past it. I'd accepted the fact they were never getting back together, and Since Francesca was in a good place their break up didn't seem to matter anymore. Slowly, things were returning to the way they used to be.

"There's truly nothing to say. Last night I met this girl on the subway. We talked for a little bit and then she spent the night. This morning we went our separate ways."

"Why were you on the subway?"

"Had to visit a client in Brooklyn."

"And that's it? You'll never see her again?"

"Honestly, I'm not even sure what her name was. It was something exotic, one of those names you can't pronounce." He said it with bitterness, like his conquest made him feel worse rather than better.

"If you're this miserable why don't you—"

"Please don't go there." He held up his hand to silence me. "She and I are never getting back together, even if she does live in the city. That's just how it is."

"I would accept that...if you weren't so depressed without her."

He looked down into his beer. "I don't deserve her and I never will. End of story."

"I don't know...you still do a lot of stuff for her."

"That's different. I can give her the world and I still wouldn't deserve her."

I wasn't sure why I kept bringing up this subject when I understood it less and less.

"One day she'll get married and forget about me entirely. And I'll be happy when that day comes."

She'd been a lot happier lately, and I knew she would find a good guy someday. But I suspected she would never forget about Hawke no matter how much time had passed. I knew I wouldn't forget about Marie no matter what happened between us.

"Let me know when they're done with the remodel. I'd like to see it."

"Sure. It'll be a few weeks."

Friday

"Keep me posted."

I kept glancing at my phone, waiting for Marie to text me when she was going to bed.

Hawke noticed my behavior. "A watched pot never boils."

"Am I making it that obvious?"

"Axel, you've been making it obvious for an entire year."

CHAPTER TWENTY-SIX

Love In Bloom

Marie

"It's weird seeing you around here." Francesca teased me every time I walked through the door. I was at Axel's place more than I was at the apartment, so it didn't surprise me.

"You must be enjoying it. Having the place all to yourself." I set my bag of dirty clothes on the couch.

"You would think, but not really. It's actually a little lonely..."

Now I felt guilty.

She turned off the TV. "Everything still great with Axel?"

"It's perfect." There was no better way to describe it. He treated me like a queen, pampered me like a goddess, and he looked at me like I was the greatest piece of art the world had ever seen.

"I told you." A triumphant look was in her eyes. She loved being right—and making sure everyone knew it.

"Alright. I'll give you the win." I didn't have a problem doing that because I was so happy.

"He's wrapped so damn tight around your finger." She shook her head. "I've never seen a man whipped harder."

Hawke was pretty whipped when they were together. "What have you been up to?"

"Met some guy the other night. We went out for a few drinks then stayed at his place." Francesca was returning to herself in stages. Now she was almost exactly where she used to be before Hawke stepped into the picture.

"How'd that go?"

"He was hot and good in bed but I don't see it going anywhere."

She slept with him? She really had jumped back on the horse. "Why not?"

"He's a hotdog vendor." She cringed. "That's just not sexy to me."

"You want to open a bakery."

"That's different. My store won't be outside on a street corner. And hotdog vendors pick their noses…"

"Says who?"

"I don't know…people."

"If you didn't like him why did you sleep with him?"

"I didn't know about the hotdog vendor thing until after I slept with him. If he told me before…it probably wouldn't have happened."

I laughed. "I didn't realize you were so picky."

"I'm not. But that didn't get my fire burning, you know?"

"So, when is the shop going to be open?"

"I don't know…not for a few weeks. Now I need to start finding some employees."

"You need to jump on that."

"Yeah…I just don't know where to start."

"Well, I can help. Axel can too."

"When you say help do you mean actually help?" she asked sarcastically. "Or just make out the whole time?"

"Hey, you want help or not?" I put my hand on my hip and gave her attitude.

She knew she was in the lower position. "I'll take whatever I can get."

Friday

"What have you decided to name the place anyway?"

She looked down at her hands for a second before she looked at me again. "The Muffin Girl."

I remembered the times when Hawke called her that. It eventually became shortened to Muffin. It wasn't clear if she picked that name because of him or because she thought it was appropriate. And I didn't ask.

She answered on her own. "I can't shake the name off. It's fitting and it has a ring to it. Honestly, the name will always remind me of him but that's not a bad thing. When I think about him, it doesn't hurt anymore."

"For what it's worth, I like it."

"I do too."

"It gives it a small town feeling in a big city. People will like that."

"Probably."

"It's a good marketing strategy."

"So...when do you think you guys can help me?"

"Well, I'm available now. And I know if I called Axel he'll be here in a heartbeat."

She chuckled. "To suck your neck."

"He'll be productive. Of the three of us, he wants you to succeed the most." He took out a loan in his own name just to help her get started. If that wasn't a declaration of belief then I didn't know what was.

"Then give him a call."

***

We worked at Axel's apartment since it was four times the size of mine. There was a lot more room, and our elbows weren't wedged in each other's sides.

"I like this girl." Axel held up the application. "She worked in a bakery for four years. She's done pastries, cookies, pies...everything you can think of."

"What about wedding cakes?" Francesca asked.

Axel skimmed through the application. "Doesn't look like it..."

"So strange." Francesca grabbed another slice of pizza from the box. "I can't believe not a single person has any experience."

"Maybe they already work full time somewhere else," Axel said. "You haven't posted any full time positions."

"Well, I will. I just can't afford it right this second."

"I'm just saying..." He held up both hands and retreated. "You can't expect competitive people to apply if you don't offer competitive salaries."

"I'm a bakery, not an investment company," Francesca argued.

"Whatever." Axel kept going through the pile. "This guy is good. He worked as a cook in a few diners then as a chef in a high-end café downtown. I think he'll be good for the lunch portion of the bakery, sandwiches and stuff like that."

I took the application and read through it. "He sounds great on paper."

"Alright," Francesca said as she chewed. "He's in."

Axel grabbed another folder and handed it to her. "These are all the manufacturers I could find that will help with your products. Flour, sugar, eggs, etc. If we buy in bulk the price is pretty cheap."

Francesca looked through the items. "I care more about quality than quantity."

"They're good," Axel argued. "They are suppliers to all the big places in Italy. Shipping will be a bitch but your stuff will be so delicious it won't matter."

Francesca nodded as she kept reading through it. "What about the shipping costs?"

"That's a little pricey..." Axel shrugged. "But it'll be worth it."

I felt like I wasn't contributing to this at all, but I really had no input. Axel and Francesca were good with numbers. I was good with words.

While Francesca was occupied with the list, Axel turned to me. He gave me a smolder then rubbed his leg against mine under the table. His look was as easy to read as a book.

Francesca didn't look up. "Please don't start making out."

"How did you know?" Axel snapped.

"I can just tell." She flipped through the pages. "Alright. I'm in. With all the competition in the city, I definitely have to be different. Quality product is key to that."

Axel kept staring at me, but his affectionate look disappeared. "I have a great idea."

"What?" I suspected this had something to do with me.

"Marie, can you write something about The Muffin Girl when it opens?" he asked. "Even just a paragraph? Tons of women read Prada."

"I can't just write anything I want." If that were the case, I'd have the best job ever.

"Maybe you could pass it along to your boss?" Axel asked.

"I haven't been there long enough to stick out my neck like that." I turned to Francesca. "I'm sorry. You know I would if I could."

"It's really okay," she said. "No hard feelings."

Axel fell silent, still brainstorming.

"Alright," Francesca said. "I'll call these people for interviews and get the ball rolling. We'll need to order our first batch of ingredients so they'll get in here in time. We still need a marketing strategy. There's not much point in having a bakery if no one knows about it."

"I'll keep thinking."

"Yeah," Axel said. "We'll come up with something."

***

Francesca left and I stayed with Axel. I didn't have much choice in the matter because Axel refused to let me leave. He wanted me by his side at all times—not that I minded.

"How about I take you out to dinner?" Axel pulled me onto his lap as he sat on the couch. "Somewhere nice? I can feel you up in the bathroom."

"How romantic..."

"Come on, you hungry?"

"A little. But I don't really want to go out." I straddled his hips and massaged his chest.

"That works for me." He grinned from ear-to-ear. "I can order another pizza."

I'd been eating out way too much. Ever since I started this new job and got back together with Axel all we ever did was eat and screw. "Can we just eat something here?"

"Sure...but I don't have anything."

"You never go to the grocery store?"

"Not unless I need toilet paper and beer."

"Well, I'll have to make more stops at the store."

"You do have a key..."

"Is that the reason you gave it to me?"

He shrugged. "It may be one of the reasons."

I crossed my arms over my chest.

"Baby, you know I'm kidding." He pulled me against him and kissed my neck. "You know, we can just eat you instead."

"I doubt that's very nutritious."

"I disagree." He kept kissing me.

Someone knocked on the front door and shattered the heat between us.

"Do you think that's Francesca?"

"No. It's probably Hawke." He sighed before he lifted me and returned me to the couch.

"Why is he here?"

"I asked for his help."

His help with what?

"What's up, man?" Axel fist-bumped him before he let him inside. "Thanks for stopping by."

"No problem." Hawke walked into the living room with his hands in his pockets. "Hey, Marie."

"Hey." Despite the sweet things he did, I would never truly look at him the same way. He hurt Francesca a lot when he dropped her like a hat. As her best friend, it was impossible for me to forget the destruction he left behind.

"Glad you two are back together." He sat on the other couch and unbuttoned the front of his jacket.

"Thanks. Me too."

Axel jumped over the couch and landed on the cushion beside me.

"What's going on with the business?" Hawke asked.

What business?

"We found a supplier, employees, the name, and almost everything else," Axel explained. "But we're missing one crucial point."

Why was Axel telling Hawke about Francesca's bakery? Like he was a part of it?

"What is it?" Hawke asked.

"Marketing," Axel said. "None of us have any idea what to do. If this were a small town, just being open would be enough. But in a big city like this, we need to do something. I was hoping you had some insight or connection that could help us."

"Hold on," I said. "I'm confused here. Why is Hawke participating in this? Last time I checked this was Francesca's business and she doesn't need his help to get the place off the ground." She was doing just fine without him and didn't need him to intervene now.

Hawke remained collected. "Marie, I just want to help."

"She doesn't need your help. She's got us." Hawke hadn't done anything to me personally, and he did attempt to put Axel and I back together—twice. But I was still loyal to my friend.

"Baby." Axel moved his hand to my thigh. "It's okay."

"No, it's not okay," I snapped. "Francesca can handle her own. She doesn't need anyone to do anything for her. So take your connections somewhere else. She doesn't need your pity."

Hawke shook his head slightly. "I definitely don't pity her."

"Baby, just let it go." Axel lowered his voice even though Hawke could still hear everything. "Trust me on this."

"Trust you on what?" I countered. "Hawke has no business being a part of this. I'm her best friend and you're her brother, who got the loan for her. What has Hawke done? Not a damn thing. So why is he here?"

Axel sighed before he turned to Hawke, silently communicating with him.

All Hawke did was shake his head.

What was I missing here?

"What does it matter?" Axel asked. "If there's anything else we can do to help Francesca, we should do it."

"I can assure you she wouldn't want Hawke's help." She was over him, at least for the most part, and I knew she wouldn't want him to be involved in this.

"He didn't ask me," Hawke said. "I volunteered."

"It's one thing to check on her and make sure she's okay, but this is different," I argued. "It's just like what I said before. You can't have it both ways. You can't not be with her but still be involved in her life, especially without her knowledge."

"Would it be better if I made my presence known?" Hawke didn't say it coldly, but his underlying irritation was bubbling. "That I was constantly there, inhibiting her from moving on with her life? Or is it better that I lurk in the shadows so she never thinks about me?"

When he put it like that I didn't have an argument.

"All I want is for Francesca to succeed," Hawke said. "I have no other motive. She doesn't need to know I was involved. No one gets hurt."

"I still feel like I'm betraying her." I was more loyal to Francesca than anyone else in my life.

"You aren't," Axel said. "You know I'm protective of Francesca too. I wouldn't be doing this if I didn't think it was okay."

Hawke watched me, waiting for me to get on board.

Friday

Since they both made a compelling argument and I was going to lose no matter what, I agreed. "Fine."

Axel rubbed the back of his neck like he was nervous. "Okay. What do you think we should do?"

"I have a friend at *The New York Times*," Hawke said. "I think I can get her to write an article for me. But she'll need to try the food and pastries herself, otherwise she won't have anything to write about."

How did he have connections like this? "How are you going to get a writer for the *New York Times* to write about a significant bakery in Manhattan?"

Hawke wouldn't meet my gaze. He pulled out his phone and searched his contacts. "Which means you'll have to arrange something, Axel. I'll ask her to keep my name out of and pretend you're familiar with each other."

"I can do that," Axel said.

"I'm guessing Francesca can make everything in the apartment," Hawke said. "So she doesn't need the bakery."

"I'm sure that's fine," Axel said.

"Great," Hawke said. "I'll call her tomorrow."

E. L. Todd

"Is there anything else you can think of?" Axel asked.

"I know a guy who runs Sprinkles," Hawke said. "I can ask him to cross promote with her. He's been my client for the past year and we have a good relationship. If I cut out one of my fees, he'll probably do it."

"That sounds perfect." Getting the attention of regulars from another bakery was golden. If she had that and the article, she would be a success—guaranteed. "Looks like everything should work out."

"It will," Hawke said. "I'll use her muffins, pastries, and coffee at my meetings with clients. When they ask about the food, which they will, I'll hand out her business card."

I was beginning to understand how vital Hawke was. Since he worked with different kinds of people, mainly wealthy ones, all over New York he knew all the right people. Now I felt a little guilty for telling him off earlier.

"Excellent," Axel said as he rubbed his hands together. "It looks like we have the perfect plan underway. That shop is going to be the biggest bakery in the city."

Hawke chuckled. "More like in the country."

***

Friday

When the alarm went off Axel tightened his arm around my waist and sprinkled kisses up and down my arm. He kissed my neck then the groove along my spine. He woke me up quietly, his lips more soothing than the irritating sound of the alarm.

"I hate working." I used to be excited to go to Prada every single day. But now when I had to get up in the morning I could hardly get out of bed. I had a gorgeous man to share my bed so I had even less of a reason to get up.

"Quit." He pressed his lips to my hairline.

"I need food." I kept my eyes closed because I was still too tired to open them.

"I can feed you."

"I need clothes...shoes. God, I need shoes."

He chuckled into my ear. "I can buy all those things for you."

"No..." I finally opened my eyes and sat up. "I like buying them myself. I just don't like working for them."

"Well...you could work for me." He pulled me against his chest and kissed my chest. "Cook and clean for me. Take care of me. And I'll pay you for all the hard work you do."

"Sounds like a housewife gig."

"It is. And I have an open position."

I rolled my eyes and got out of bed. "Nah."

He continued to lay in bed, the sheets bunched around his waist. His hard chest and chiseled arms were inviting, silently calling me back to bed. "Come on. I think you'd be a great housewife."

"Ugh. I'd be terrible at it."

"How so? You already cook and clean for me anyway."

I walked to the sink and grabbed my toothbrush. "Now I'm starting to think you aren't joking."

"Who said I was?" He watched my expression in the mirror.

It was hard to believe there was a time when he couldn't tell me he loved me. Now he told me every night before bed. And he showed it every second of the day. "I'm getting into the shower."

"Can I join you?"

"Nope." I walked into the bathroom and got the shower running. The warm water fell on me, waking me up.

Axel joined me a moment later. He grabbed a bar of soap and began to rub me down, lathering the soap into my skin. He massaged my body, making me fall asleep even though I was trying to wake up.

"I never pictured you as the clingy type."

"Clingy?" he asked. "I'm not clingy."

"I don't think you understand the definition."

"I'm just a man in love with a woman." He turned me around then picked me up, holding me in the shower. "Is that really a bad thing?"

"No." I wrapped my arms around his neck.

"I was hoping you would say that." He held me up by my ass and kissed me slowly, the water running down our bodies. The soap was washed away and the time passed. Both of us were going to be late to work but neither one of us seemed to care.

***

"I can't believe this." Francesca sat inside the bakery with her pasties placed in airtight containers. "I made four different batches of everything just to make sure it was absolutely perfect."

"It will be perfect." The bakery was nearly completed. All the counters and kitchens had been built but now they were missing the tile in the rear. The grand opening was just in two weeks and time was running down.

"What if she doesn't like them?" Francesca asked.

"She will," I said. "Name one person who's tried your stuff and didn't like it."

"Well, if they didn't like it they wouldn't tell me," she argued.

"I would," I said honestly.

"Me too," Axel added.

Francesca kept eyeing the window, waiting for the reporter to arrive. "Axel, how the hell did you arrange this? How do you know her?"

He shrugged. "I meet a lot of people through work."

"But that would mean you just met her," she said. "How did you get her to do this favor for you?"

I felt bad for Axel. He was being put right on the spot.

"What can I say?" he said casually. "I'm charming."

Francesca dropped the subject so she must have believed him.

A woman walked up to the door, wearing a skintight dress with a pink blouse. Her hair was in big curls that trailed down her chest. She was the definition of a bombshell. She had the perfect body, the perfect legs—the perfect everything. Now it became abundantly clear how Hawke knew her. And I was sick just thinking about it.

She took a look around before she approached our table.

"Frankie, you got this," I whispered. "Be confident."

She strode to our table like she owned the place. "You must be Francesca." She extended her hand.

"Yes—The Muffin Girl." Francesca put on a nice smile and didn't seem nervous at all. "Thanks for meeting me today."

"No problem," she said in a husky voice. "I'm Amy and I've heard nothing but good things." She turned to Axel, narrowing her eyes.

"It's nice to see you again," he said proactively as he shook her hand. "Thanks for coming down."

"Of course," she said. "It's always nice to see you, Axel."

Axel wrapped his arm around me. "This is my girlfriend. I love her."

Francesca tried not to laugh.

I couldn't hold mine back. "But people call me Marie." I shook her hand. "I think you'll be impressed by everything Francesca has created."

"I'm sure I will." She took a seat and effortlessly flipped her hair over one shoulder.

Axel kept his arm around me, practically squeezing me.

Francesca poured the cup of coffee. "How do you take it?"

"Black is fine," Amy answered.

Francesca handed her the cup then opened her Tupperware. One by one, she explained each pastry, detailing the ingredients and the process of making it.

Amy took a bite of each pastry, and judging her expression she seemed genuinely surprised with each bite. She savored every piece then sipped her coffee. "Honestly, I'm impressed."

Francesca's face lit up. "I've been baking my entire life. I didn't think my dream of owning a bakery would ever come true—until now."

"With a product like this, I'm sure you'll be fine." She grabbed her notepad and made a few notes.

"Would you like a tour?" Francesca asked. "It's not completely done but the essentials are in place."

"I'd love to," Amy said. "I can ask you some questions along the way."

Francesca took Amy behind the counters and showed her where everything would be placed. Then she guided her to the back of the bakery and showed her the various kitchens and wedding cake station.

Axel relaxed when Amy was gone.

"You can chill out now."

"What?" he asked innocently.

"It's okay if you think she's hot."

"But I don't think she's hot."

I rolled my eyes.

"What? I don't."

"Then why are you all over me?" I asked.

"I just don't want you to think that I think she's hot."

I gave him a blank stare.

"I know she's pretty and I didn't want you to think I was into her."

"But you do think she's hot if you noticed she was hot."

"And I didn't want her to hit on me. I saw the way she looked at me when she first walked in here."

This conversation was stupid so I let it drop. "Whatever."

"I'm not lying."

"You sound guilty. I don't care if you check out other women. I check out other guys."

"But I don't check out—" His mouth suddenly shut. "What? You check out other guys?"

"Sometimes," I said with a shrug.

"I don't look at other women."

"Sure…"

"Marie, I'm not lying." He grew defensive and even a little angry. "Look, I'll tell you how it is every time. And I'm telling you, I don't do that."

That part was true. He never lied and he had no reason to start now. "Okay. I believe you."

"Now you need to stop checking out other dudes. Your eyes are for me only."

I never thought I'd find clinginess to be attractive, but it looked good on him. "Okay. I'll stop."

"I mean it," he said. "No eye candy for you."

I rolled my eyes because he was being ridiculous.

Amy and Francesca returned a few moments later.

"I know I haven't written the article yet, but rest assured it will be a good one." Amy shook her hand. "It was a pleasure meeting you, Muffin Girl."

"Thank you so much." Francesca opened the door for her.

"And you can count on me as a customer." Amy winked before she walked out.

Francesca shut the door then came back to us. "That went well."

"I told you that you would rock it," I said, not bothering to hide my triumph.

"She said she liked the food and thinks the bakery is cute," Francesca said. "I have a good feeling about this."

"Just don't hire any hot guys," Axel said darkly. "Since Marie likes to check them out."

Francesca returned to the chair and boxed up her things. "Did you tell him about Hawke?"

I had no idea what she was talking about so I gave her a blank stare.

Axel narrowed his eyes on her. "Sorry?"

"About how Marie had the hots for him before he and I met. He would come into The Grind a few times a week and Marie—"

"Stop. Talking. Now." Of all the things I expected her to say, that was not it. Since that had never popped up I thought it was buried in the past. Apparently, it wasn't.

E. L. Todd

Axel's expression didn't change, but there was a storm brewing underneath. Since he didn't like it when I checked out strangers, he certainly wouldn't like it when I checked out his best friend. "Hawke…"

Francesca didn't realize the devastating blow she just made. "Yeah. She called dibs on him before he and I started talking."

I gave her a venomous glare. "Frankie, shut the hell up."

"What?" she asked innocently. "What's the big deal? It was a long time ago."

He rubbed the back of his neck before he gripped his temple. "Let me get this straight…you wanted Hawke first?"

"Not first," I argued. "He used to come into The Grind and I thought he was cute. That's it. Nothing else."

"But you wanted to ask him out." Axel wouldn't even look at me. His head was about to explode.

Francesca finally caught on. "You can't actually be mad about that, Axel. It was a long time ago, and it was before you and Marie even saw each other."

"Stay out of this," he snapped.

Francesca knew she needed to give both of us space. She gathered her things and left the

361

shop, leaving the keys behind so we could lock up whenever we were done, not that there was a reason to lock up. There was nothing to steal.

Now that we were alone, Axel blew up. "So you wanted him? He was the one you originally wanted but couldn't have?"

"You're blowing this out of proportion. I never asked him out and he never asked me out. So there was never a time when I couldn't have him. When Francesca started dating him, I didn't care in the least."

He left the chair then started pacing in silence.

Could he seriously be mad about this?

"You wanted my best friend, not me."

"Axel, you weren't even in the picture at this point. I didn't even know the two of you knew each other."

"That doesn't matter."

"Yes, it does matter." I understood why he was uncomfortable but he was blowing it out of proportion and I didn't like that one bit. "I'm sure you've checked out one of my friends and thought they were cute."

"No, I've never had the hots for any of them. How would you feel if I did?"

"I wouldn't care."

"Yes, you would," he snapped. "Don't sit there and act like you wouldn't." He gave me a dark stare before he began to pace again.

"Axel, just calm down."

"Calm down?" he hissed. "I just found out the woman I love wanted my best friend first. How do you think that makes me feel?"

"Axel, nothing happened. Not once did we talk about it. We literally had no interaction."

"But that's not the point. You wanted him in your bed—not me."

"There was no competition, Axel. You weren't around."

"But we got together just a few weeks after that. I'm basically a rebound."

I wanted to scream because this was so ridiculous. "You're overreacting."

"Maybe. Or maybe you just don't get it." He marched around me and burst through the front door.

"Axel!"

He kept going, determined to get away from me as quickly as possible.

Friday

CHAPTER TWENTY-SEVEN

Betrayal

Axel

"Open the damn door." I pounded my fists as hard as I could.

The door finally flew open. Hawke stood in his sweatpants. His hair was messed up like he'd been rolling around in his bed. He was shirtless and sweaty. "What the hell is your problem?"

I barged in without being invited. "My problem? You're my problem." I pushed him hard against the wall.

Hawke collided with the wall but didn't retaliate. His eyes showed the blood rage pounding deep inside him. "I'm going to let that go because you're upset about something. But touch me again, motherfucker, and I'll make you regret it."

"Marie. She wanted you first."

His anger disappeared instantly, replaced by confusion. "What are you talking about?"

"You used to come into The Grind all the time and she had a crush on you. She wanted to ask you out but Francesca got to you first." I watched his expression, trying to figure out if he knew anything about that.

He kept a stoic expression.

"You knew she was into you."

"Axel, it was a long time ago."

"I can't believe this..." I took a step back, feeling sick to my stomach.

"Look, nothing happened. She never asked me out and I never asked her out. I'd had my eye on Francesca from the beginning. No offense to Marie, but she didn't stand a chance."

"But she wanted you...before she wanted me."

"And you haven't wanted other women before Marie?" he asked incredulously. "Are you five?"

"It's different. You're my best friend."

"It was just a crush, Axel. She thought I was cute and that was the extent of her feelings. She can barely stand to be in the same room as me now. She doesn't look at me like that anymore. The second Francesca and I started talking, Marie forgot about me."

I still felt like shit. "How did you know she was into you?"

He put his hands on his hips. "I don't know...she'd stare at me a lot. Anytime I would order she was always quiet, giggling at anything I said. Stuff like that."

Hawke and I looked nothing alike, so the fact she was attracted to him made me doubt my appearance. I crossed my arms over my chest and leaned against the wall.

"Axel, don't be like this." He came closer to me when he knew I'd calmed down. "You're reading way too much into it."

"How would you feel if Francesca wanted one of your friends before she wanted you?"

Like always, he changed the second she was brought up. "I wouldn't like it at all. But I would get over it. Because what she and I had was much stronger than the physical attraction she had for someone else. There's no reason to be threatened by me, Axel. What you guys have is real. You guys love each other and want to spend the rest of your lives together. How could you possibly care about any other guy Marie has ever been with? You're the man she loves."

Friday

Despite those emotional words I was still angry. I felt betrayed, like someone stabbed me in the back. I didn't expect to be Marie's one and only, but I thought she only noticed me and not my best friend. "I've got to go..." I turned back to the door. "I'm sorry for bothering you."

"Axel, come on."

I kept walking. "Good night."

He followed me into the hallway. "Let it go. You're upset over nothing."

My shoulders slouched and felt a million times too heavy. I was sick to my stomach. I felt like my arms and legs had been ripped off. Everything hurt. It was as if Marie cheated on me even though she hadn't. It felt like my world had ended.

***

I steered clear of Marie as much as possible. I didn't answer her phone calls and I didn't go back to my apartment because I knew she had a key. I ended up checking into a hotel room with a suitcase.

I wasn't ready to talk to her.

She left me voicemails and text messages, all of which went unanswered. Most of the time I just deleted them without knowing what they said. By the end of the week I was still upset. I felt wounded, like someone jabbed a knife into my lungs.

By the end of the week she stopped calling. Maybe she got the hint that I needed some space. Suffocating me with her apologies wouldn't change the way I felt. But I didn't know what could change the way I felt. If it were anyone else but Hawke it might have been different. He was the good-looking playboy all the girls were interested in. I thought Marie only noticed me—and not him.

Francesca's shop was about to open and I knew I couldn't ignore her forever. She needed my help as well as my support. If I missed that opening day I'd regret it forever.

I called her the night before the big day.

She answered it coldly. "What do you want?"

I knew whose side she was on. "Is everything ready for tomorrow?"

"Yes." She was giving me the cold shoulder—bad.

"Do you need me for anything?"

"No."

"Frankie, come on. I want tomorrow to go over well."

Friday

"And it will. Now if you excuse me, I should go." She hung up before I could get another word in.

I lay back on my bed and stared up at the ceiling.

CHAPTER TWENTY-EIGHT

Finished

Marie

We were over.

I thought everything was great and perfect, but then we had to hit that bump in the road. Axel was upset over something that happened before we even slept together, so it was impossible for me to change it. And it was unfair to hold it against me.

But I still felt guilty for hurting him.

He disappeared off the map. He never went back to his apartment, and he never answered my phone calls or messages. It was abundantly clear our relationship was over. It was beautiful while it lasted, and I never expected to be the reason it wouldn't work out.

Caught me by surprise.

Despite the pain I was in, I put on a bright smile for Francesca. Her shop was opening and I wanted to be as supportive as possible. Today, my pain was irrelevant. Her biggest dream was coming true.

I arrived at the shop at seven in the morning with a cup of coffee in my hands. Francesca was having her grand opening, cutting the ribbon for the cameras that had been scheduled to appear—thanks to Hawke. I didn't expect Axel to be there. Normally, he would be there in a heartbeat. But since I was there, I knew he would stay away.

The workers were already inside, perfecting the final pastries that would be for sale as soon as the doors opened. Customers hovered outside, waiting to get their cups of gourmet coffee. I stood off to the side, witnessing all of this as another bystander.

That's when I spotted him.

Axel was on the side of the entryway, wearing a suit and tie like he planned to go to work after the grand opening. His eyes were on me and he watched me intently. His expression was unreadable.

I looked away, refusing to make eye contact with him. He dumped me coldly over something so stupid. Yes, I was attracted to Hawke at one point but that didn't make me a bad person. I stepped aside and let Francesca have him because I knew they should be together.

But he wouldn't let it go.

Axel walked around the crowd, slowly coming my way.

I didn't look at him, sipping my coffee and waiting for Francesca to cut the beautiful yellow ribbon tied between the doors.

When he came to my side the air changed around both of us. I felt the tension in the air, the anger as well as the sorrow.

Without looking at him, I said, "Today is about Francesca. So, whatever you want to say can wait until another time."

He stood beside me, his hands in his pockets. "I just wanted to apologize for my behavior. It was childish and stupid."

I never expected an apology. He seemed too upset to see reason.

"I shouldn't have ignored you like that. It was wrong."

There was nothing else I could do besides forgive him, so that's what I did. "I forgive you." I sipped my coffee and kept watching the crowd. They seemed anxious to get out of the sun and into the cute bakery.

Axel grabbed my coffee and tossed it in the garbage.

Friday

"Hey!"

He turned me toward him. "I'll buy you another one. But right now I want you to look at me."

"Why?" I pulled my elbow out of his grasp. "What's there to see?"

"You accepted my apology but it doesn't seem like you mean it."

"I do mean it. But what do you expect me to do? Smile and hug you?" When people broke up, they steered clear of one another. I was only making an exception right now because it was Francesca's big day.

"Yes, actually." He cupped my face with both of his hands, touching me just the way he used to. "I just got jealous and let it get to my head...it was stupid. I've never been in a relationship before so I've never experienced jealousy. Now that I know what it is I recognize it. It was wrong of me to hold that against you. Actually, it was stupid. I want you to know I'm sorry and I learned from my mistake."

I felt myself melt at his touch—like always.

"I understand if you're still mad at me. I shouldn't have ignored you like that. That's what I'm most sorry for."

Feeling his cold rejections stung. Of course, it did.

"Baby, do you forgive me?"

"I don't know...you just broke up with me." How could I sweep that under the rug—again?"

His eyes narrowed. "Broke up with you? What are you talking about?"

"When you ignored me for a week straight, I could only assume."

He closed his eyes and sighed like he was in pain. "No...that's not what that was. I just wanted space. Marie, even if you cheated on me, I wouldn't leave you. That makes me pathetic, I know. And please don't cheat on me now that you know that. But it's the truth. Baby, I'm never going to let you go again—no matter how angry I get. I'm sorry for scaring you."

I was relieved I'd misread him.

"Please tell me you're still mine." The sincerity in his voice broke my heart.

"Always."

He pressed his forehead to mine and closed his eyes, releasing a deep sigh. "I'm sorry I broke my promise to you. I didn't mean to."

"Axel, it's normal for couples to fight in relationships. It happens. So don't promise something like that. But you can promise to work it out with me—every time."

He opened his eyes again. "Yeah, I guess that's a better compromise."

I cupped his face and kissed him. "I love you."

"I love you too." He kissed me again before he pressed his lips against my forehead. "So much it scares me sometimes." His arms wrapped around me, forming steel cages, and he held me into his chest.

"It scares me too."

"Hey, if you guys are done I'm going to open my bakery now." Francesca stood holding an enormous pair of scissors. She was giving us both the stink eye since we were making out on the corner.

"Sorry." I grabbed Axel's hand and we joined her in front of the doors. Axel grabbed the ribbon and made sure the tension was tight so she'd have an easy time cutting it. Once the shot was timed with the photographers she cut the rope.

And The Muffin Girl finally opened.

CHAPTER TWENTY-NINE

The Next Step
Axel

I was grateful Marie forgave me and my little tantrum. I got upset quicker than I meant to, and then everything came pouring out. Before I knew it, I was waist deep in shit. She could have broken it off with me and had every right to.

But she didn't.

Like every Sunday night, Marie packed all of her dirty clothes and shoes into her duffel bag. It was a ritual we practiced every single week. She prepared to return to the apartment she shared with Francesca, and I'd be sleeping alone most nights until the weekend returned.

I hated it.

"Baby, don't go." I grabbed her by the hips and dragged her back to bed. "I hate it when you leave."

Friday

"I hate it too." She lay underneath me on the bed.

"Then stay." Every time I said goodbye it was actually painful. I wanted to share everything with her—share my life. My hand fisted her hair and I kissed her, doing my best to seduce her.

"Axel, I need to do laundry and get ready for work."

"I have a washer and dryer."

"But I have other stuff to wash—like my bed."

"You don't even sleep in it."

"That's not the point."

"Then let me come over." If I had to get up an hour early to make sure I made it to work on time, then so be it. It was worth it.

"Francesca is still there."

"Kick her out. She has a job now."

"She's welcome to stay as long as she wants."

I growled under my breath.

"Babe, I know this sucks. But it's not the end of the world."

To me it was. "The best part of this relationship is having you by my side every second of the day. How am I supposed to sleep if you aren't with me? It's just not the same."

"I know but we have other responsibilities."

"Who cares?"

"And I can't get much writing done when I'm here."

"Then we'll turn the spare bedroom into an office. You can work here whenever you want."

"Like you'd let me. You'd be kissing my neck and feeling me up the whole time."

I smiled. "Like you wouldn't like that."

"I would like it. That's the problem."

I was tired of begging her at the end of every week. When she said I was clingy she was dead on. I was clingy—with her. She made me happy and I didn't want her to be anywhere else but here. Was it that strange?

She moved from under me then returned to her feet. "I'm sorry, Axel."

I didn't like it when I didn't get my way. "Let me walk you." I didn't like it when she walked home alone in the city after dark. Even if she took a cab or stuck to well-lit areas it made me uneasy.

She didn't object to that—which was smart.

***

Friday

I walked her to her door and prepared for the dreadful goodbye. "I had a great time this weekend."

"Me too."

I wrapped my arms around her waist and rested them on the small of her back. We went out to dinner and for some drinks on Friday night, and then we went to the movies on Saturday. Today, we just lay around the house and made love nonstop. But now the weekend was over. "I want every day to be the weekend."

"I think everyone does."

I cupped her face and gave her a soft kiss. Whenever our mouths touched I felt alive, like I could do anything. It invigorated me with life and passion. I'd never kissed another woman and felt that way before.

She pulled away and rubbed her nose against mine. "I love you."

"I love you too."

She got the door unlocked then walked inside. She gave me a quick wave before she shut the door.

I stood there, staring at the peephole. My hands moved into my pockets and I felt the ache in my chest the second she was gone. Now I would return to my empty apartment, the one I shared with no one, and I would tried to get some sleep despite how futile it was.

And then I realized how much I didn't want to do that.

I'd rather sleep outside her door than go home alone.

I didn't have a problem being on my own. But once I felt that connection with Marie I never wanted to let go. I wanted to be near her always. When I came home from work I wanted her to be there.

I always wanted to be there.

I opened the door and walked inside, not thinking about my actions before I did them.

Marie and Francesca were talking in the living room. Marie was standing at the back of the couch, and she turned to me when she realized I walked inside without knocking. "Axel, is everything okay?"

"Knock, asshole," Francesca snapped.

I came closer to her, ignoring both of the things they just said. "Move in with me."

Francesca covered her mouth and gasped.

Marie stood there in shock, her eyes wide.

"I know it's a little fast but I don't care. When I come home every day I want you to be there. I'm tired of seeing you pack up your things just to return to this apartment with Francesca. I'm tired of sharing you. Please move in with me." This was the perfect solution to all my problems. It was too soon for me to propose but this was doable. A lot of couples moved in together before they got married. Marie and I never talked about it, but I knew she was the woman I'd spend the rest of my life with. "Francesca can have this apartment and you can just move your stuff to my place. You're there all the time anyway." It made perfect sense.

Francesca stared at Marie and waited for her to give an answer.

Her silence unnerved me. Was this something she wasn't ready for? Did she have doubts? Was it because of the fight we had a few weeks ago? "Baby?" If she said no I'd be hurt. But I'd do my best to mask the pain on my features.

"Yes."

All the anxiety left my body when I heard that one single word. A grin stretched my face and I felt lighter than air. She actually said yes. I closed the gap between us and hugged her tightly.

"Yes, I'll move in with you."

"Awe..." Francesca watched us from the couch. "My brother...the hopeless romantic."

"Shut up." I grabbed a pillow and threw it at her.

"You're sure you want to do this?" Marie leaned back and looked into my face.

"Absolutely. Completely. Undeniably."

"I'll be there every day..."

'That's what I'm hoping for."

She finally smiled, her happiness matching mine. "Then let's do it."

Friday

EPILOGUE

Axel

"I'm fucking nervous as fucking hell." I kept pacing the apartment, checking the front pocket of my jacket over and over.

Hawke eyed me, a grin on his face. "Just calm down."

"You calm down."

He raised an eyebrow. "If I were any calmer, I'd be asleep."

I rubbed the back of my neck, feeling my heart slam into my chest. "She's going to be home any minute and we're heading to the airport."

"Just do it exactly as we rehearsed it."

"What if I blow it?" I was going to scuff up my floor if I kept walking like this.

"You won't."

"You don't know me very well…"

Friday

"Think of it this way. No matter what you say or how badly you do it, she's going to say yes."

"You think?" That was the only good thing he said to me.

"Yes."

Footsteps were heard on the other side of the door. "Shit, she's here. Fuck, act natural." I walked up to Hawke and put my arm around his shoulders.

"You think this is natural?" he whispered. He pushed my arm down.

Marie walked inside. "I'm so glad I'm done with work and we're going on vacation." She threw her arms up and did a little dance.

I just stared at her, too nervous to do anything else.

Hawke elbowed me in the side.

"Yeah...so excited." I was so excited my heart was about to give out.

"I'm just about to grab my stuff and we'll go." She walked up to me and gave me a big kiss. "Thanks so much for taking me on a trip."

"You're welcome, baby." I gave her ass a playful slap, trying to be normal.

She walked down the hallway and entered the bedroom.

I started to freak out all over again. "Fuck, I can't do this. I'm going to mess it up."

"You aren't going to mess it up." He gripped both of my shoulders to calm me. "Look, she loves you. She's been living with you for two years. If she hasn't left by now, she never will. All right?"

I nodded in agreement.

"The ring is gorgeous and you're a great man. She's not going to say no."

I needed any confidence boost I could get. "Thanks. Shit, asking someone to marry you is tough."

"It is," he said. "But you've got this."

***

Marie and I just finished dinner at the restaurant. It overlooked the beach and the water. The sun was about to set over the horizon, making the sky glow with hues of purple and pink.

The adrenaline kicked in.

"Want to take a walk on the beach?"

"Sure."

No one was there so it was perfect. I took her hand and guided her to the sand, walking slowly alongside her. The waves crashed on the beach and the wind blew through her hair. Her eyes were glued to the horizon, watching the sun slowly fade away.

I'd never been so terrified in my whole life. I wasn't scared she would say no. But I was scared I wouldn't do it right. What if I dropped the ring and we never found it again? What if I put the ring on the wrong hand? What if she didn't cry? So many things could go wrong.

We walked in silence, taking in the scenery. I knew I needed to do it soon before all the daylight was gone. Then she wouldn't be able to see the ring and I'd miss my chance. I'd procrastinated long enough.

"Thank you for coming with me."

"You don't need to thank me," she said with a chuckle. "Spending a week in paradise with the love of my life? Sounds like the best week of my life."

When she said things like that all the fear left my body. "You're the greatest thing that ever happened to me, you know that?"

She gave me a dazzling smile, the kind that made my heart melt. "Yeah, I think so."

I stopped walking and faced her, going with the moment. "When I picture my life without you, I don't have a life at all, just a meaningless existence. I never knew how happy I could be until I gave love a chance. All those voids I used to feel are now gone. You fixed me—put me back together."

She stared at me with soft eyes, touched by my words.

"You've given me a life I never thought I could have. Now I have the most beautiful woman in the world who loves me, who takes care of me and puts up with me. And you allow me to do the same for you. I consider myself to be the luckiest man in the world."

"Axel..."

I could do this.

I lowered myself to one knee and pulled out the box at the same time, just as I practiced for nearly a week straight.

She gasped the second she realized what was happening. "Oh my god. Oh my god. Oh my god." She clutched her chest.

"Marie Prescott, will you marry me?" I opened the lid to reveal the solitary diamond I custom designed just for her. My hands didn't shake as I held it out to her, knowing exactly what her answer would be.

And just as I hoped, she began to cry. "Axel...yes. Of course. Yes."

I slipped the ring onto her left ring finger and felt it glide on smoothly. It was a perfect fit.

"It's beautiful." She felt the band with her free hand and sniffed as the diamond caught the light.

I rose to my feet and towered over her again, realizing my own eyes were wet. I was hoping she would cry but I didn't expect to feel the same emotion. "Thank you for saying yes to me."

She wrapped her arms around me and hugged me tightly, crying quietly. "I love you, Axel."

I rested my chin on her head as I held her close to me. The waves crashed on the shore and the seagulls cried overhead. Despite the fact there were other people on the island it seemed like it was just the two of us. I asked Marie to spend the rest of her life with me and she actually said yes. "I love you too."

E. L. Todd

I hope you enjoyed reading Friday as much as I loved writing it. It would mean the world to me if you could leave a short review. It's the greatest kind of support you can give an author.

Francesca and Hawke found their happily ever after, and Axel and Marie followed in their footsteps. The universe seems to be complete. However, we're missing someone very special.

Will Kyle find his soul mate? Will Kyle find the timeless love he's been looking for? Found out in the next installment of the Timeless Series, SATURDAY.

Friday

Want To Stalk Me?

Subscribe to my newsletter for updates on new releases, giveaways, and for my comical monthly newsletter. You'll get all the dirt you need to know. Sign up today.
www.eltoddbooks.com

Facebook:
https://www.facebook.com/ELTodd42

Twitter:
@E_L_Todd

Now you have no reason not to stalk me. You better get on that.

Printed in Great Britain
by Amazon